"Sergeant Cole McKinney, Texas Ranger."

Joey licked her lips in stunned silence.

This hot-as-all-get-out bad boy was Cole McKinney? The boy who'd been shunned by the McKinney family?

And he was a law enforcement agent?

"I see the wheels turning in your head, Joey Hendricks." His husky voice skated over her raw nerve endings. "And yeah, I'm the sum of all those rotten things you were thinking. And a few more you don't even know about."

What did he know about the investigation? Something the Rangers hadn't revealed to the press?

Her hand trembled.

Was he here to arrest one or both of her parents?

RITA HERRON

JUSTICE FOR A RANGER

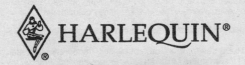

HARLEQUIN®

TORONTO • NEW YORK • LONDON
AMSTERDAM • PARIS • SYDNEY • HAMBURG
STOCKHOLM • ATHENS • TOKYO • MILAN • MADRID
PRAGUE • WARSAW • BUDAPEST • AUCKLAND

To Mallory Kane and Delores Fossen for birthing this fabulous story line and letting me be a part of it. Here's to more Rangers stories in the future....

ISBN-13: 978-0-373-88751-4
ISBN-10:   0-373-88751-5

JUSTICE FOR A RANGER

Copyright © 2007 by Rita B. Herron

ABOUT THE AUTHOR

Award-winning author Rita Herron wrote her first book when she was twelve, but didn't think real people grew up to be writers. Now she writes so she doesn't have to get a *real* job. A former kindergarten teacher and workshop leader, she traded storytelling for kids for romance, and writes romantic comedies and romantic suspense. She lives in Georgia with her own romance hero and three kids. She loves to hear from readers so please write her at P.O. Box 921225, Norcross, GA 30092-1225, or visit her Web site at www.ritaherron.com.

Books by Rita Herron

CAST OF CHARACTERS

Joey Hendricks—Guilt-ridden over her brother's disappearance/death, she will do anything to find out the truth about who kidnapped him—even if it means sending her own parents to jail.

Sergeant Cole McKinney—The bastard son of Jim McKinney has always dreamed of confronting the man who sired him, and his half brothers. But helping exonerate his father is not in his plans....

Lieutenant Zane McKinney and Sergeant Sloan McKinney—Cole's half brothers have different theories about their father's guilt.

Jim McKinney—This Texas Ranger's career and life was ruined when he was accused of murdering Lou Anne Wallace.

Leland Hendricks—Joey's father would do anything for money. But would he try to kill his wife and threaten his daughter?

Donna Hendricks—Donna blamed Leland for their toddler son's disappearance. Does she know more than she's telling?

Justin Hendricks—He was only two when he was kidnapped. Is he alive or dead?

Lou Anne Wallace Hendricks—She married Leland for his money, but couldn't give up her lovers. The police are still looking for her killer....

Rosa Ramirez—The nanny adored both Joey and Justin. Would Rosa have committed murder to stop Leland's kidnapping plan?

Governor Clayton Grange—He sent Joey to Justice to handle the media. Why is he so interested in the murders?

Chapter One

Hell must have finally frozen over in Justice, Texas.

That was the only explanation for the phone call requesting his services from his half brothers, Lieutenant Zane McKinney and Sergeant Sloan McKinney, both Texas Rangers.

As was Cole, but they had never met or asked for his help on a case before.

Not him—the bastard, bad-boy brother they all hated.

Cole traced a proud finger over the silver star he'd earned through his own blood, sweat and tears. He was a sergeant now himself. He'd made the grade with no help. No financial support or fancy education. No loving, doting parents.

Not like Zane and Sloan.

A bitter laugh rumbled from deep within his gut as he threw his clothes into a duffel bag, stepped into the hot sunshine and climbed on his Harley. Dammit. He'd been ordered to leave his current case behind, come straight out of the trenches where he'd been working a lead on a smuggling ring along the border, to assist in Justice.

Of course, his half brothers must be desperate to exonerate their father, to finally free him of the murder charges that had hung around his neck like an albatross the past sixteen years. A murder investigation that had been revived because Sarah Wallace, daughter of Lou Anne Wallace, the woman his father had slept with and had been accused of strangling with her own designer purse, had just been murdered in the same hotel room, in the same manner.

And most likely by the same person who'd killed her mother.

Bitterness swelled inside Cole as choking as the insufferable summer heat. Did his brothers actually think he gave a damn about the outcome? That he'd come running to team up with them to save their father because he wanted to see Jim McKinney's good name restored?

Jim McKinney—the father who'd abandoned him and his mother. The father who'd never acknowledged his existence. The father who had been nothing more than a sperm donor on his behalf.

The man who'd broken his mother's heart.

Barb Tyler had never married after her short affair with Jim McKinney. She'd claimed Jim had ruined her for another man. And she'd taken that love with her to her grave no more than a year after Jim McKinney's arrest. If Cole hadn't known better, he'd have thought she'd died of grief for the man's lost reputation herself.

He hated Jim for it.

Still, he was a Texas Ranger. Part of the most revered, effective investigative law enforcement agency in the world. And he was damn proud to be a lawman. God knows he'd been on a crash course to jail himself when Clete McHaven, the rancher his mother had cooked for, had caught him trying to steal from his ranch and had made him work off the debt or go to the pen.

He scrubbed a hand over his three days' growth of beard stubble, knowing he looked like hell as he strapped on his biker's helmet, cranked up the Harley's engine and tore down the driveway. Dust and pebbles spewed from his tires as he careened onto the highway. Anger and determination had him pushing the speed limit.

Not that he was in a hurry to see the long-lost family that had cast him aside as if he was a leper.

But he had a chance to prove that a real Texas Ranger didn't need book education or to be a good ole boy. That his tracking skills had earned him a spot as a top-notch lawman.

He had no intention of begging for accolades from the McKinneys, of trying to worm his way into their snotty huddle. Hell, he didn't need them or their approval.

And he would not play favorites in the investigation.

Jim McKinney had been a bastard who couldn't keep his pants zipped. And although he'd never been convicted of murder, if he had killed Lou Anne Wallace and her daughter, Cole would find out. Then he would snap the handcuffs around his wrists and haul him to jail where he belonged.

And he wouldn't think twice about who suffered when he did.

TO SOME PEOPLE GOING HOME meant reuniting with loved ones. Reliving warm memories and seeing friends. Safety.

To Joey Hendricks it meant pain and anxiety. Opening wounds that had never healed. Dealing with her own guilt over her two-year-old brother's disappearance sixteen years ago. And facing a mother and father she hadn't spoken to in years. A mother and father who hated each other.

But she did work for the governor as a special investigator and when the infamous governor of the great state of Texas said jump, she jumped.

The sign for Justice, Texas, appeared, and she grimaced. At first sight, it looked like a cozy small town in which to raise a family. A place where everyone knew his neighbor, no one ever met a stranger and they would welcome her back with loving arms.

But secrets and hatred had festered in the

town like sores that wouldn't heal. And someone wanted to keep those secrets hidden. They'd murdered Sarah Wallace to do so and had tried to kill her sister Anna and the sheriff, Carley Matheson, when they'd searched for the truth.

Her heart turned over as she passed Main Street Diner. She'd been shocked when her mother, whose total culinary skills when Joey had been growing up constituted throwing together a plate of cheese and crackers to accompany her cocktail dinner, had bought the establishment. She'd been shocked even further to learn that Donna had given up the booze and pills.

Not shocked enough to want to see her just yet, though.

Oh, it was inevitable that she face both her dysfunctional parents, but first she wanted to learn more about the investigation. Just how much and what kind of evidence did the sheriff have against Leland and Donna Hendricks?

Late evening shadows cast gray lines across the street and storefront awnings as she spotted the Matheson Inn, where she'd reserved a room. She tightened her fingers around the steering wheel and veered into a parking spot, then stared at the burned-down ruins of the Justice jail. The sign for the police department had turned to black soot. Ashes, charred black wood, burned metal all lay in rubble. Only the metal bars of the jail cell remained standing, empty and exposed, as if still waiting for a prisoner. A stark reminder that the original killer had never been incarcerated. And now he'd murdered again.

Poor Sarah Wallace... Memories of her troubled teenage years haunted her. When Lou Anne and Leland had married, Lou Anne's daughters, Sarah and Anna, had moved in with them for a short time. But they hadn't been any happier about the union than Joey, so they'd moved out shortly after. She hadn't been close to either of them, but she hated to think that Sarah had been murdered.

The stench of the fire and charred remains still filled the air, wafting in the suffocating heat as she climbed out. In front, a media crew and several locals had gathered, a camera rolling.

The very reason she was here. To control the media circus. More than one investigation had been blown because of some dim-witted or too-aggressive reporter. Innocent people had been tried and convicted in the process.

Other times the guilty had gone free.

The governor was adamant that the past not repeat itself. Lou Anne Wallace's murderer had escaped sixteen years ago, as had the person who'd kidnapped Justin, Joey's own baby brother. The town of Justice had never gotten over either event. Jim McKinney's impeccable Texas Ranger reputation had been ruined because of his affair with Lou Anne and his subsequent arrest, his family shattered because of it.

And it had destroyed what was left of Joey's already crumbling family, as well.

The governor had worked with the D.A.'s office at the time of Lou Anne's murder. Ironically Joey had been afraid that her family name would hinder her career, but the governor had given her a chance to prove herself. And she had. In fact, Governor Grange had been more of a father figure to her the past four years than her own dad had.

And he'd trusted her enough to send her here now, trusted her to be objective about the McKinneys. After all, Jim McKinney's sons were in charge of the case. Rangers investigating one of their own, especially a family member—definitely a conflict of interest.

Tucking a strand of her unruly blond hair behind one ear, she buttoned her suit jacket and headed toward the media. Harold Dennison, a reporter who had a reputation for causing trouble, stood in front of the dilapidated ruins recounting the events of the night of the fire.

"Local sheriff Carley Matheson and Texas Ranger, former sheriff of Justice and hometown boy Sergeant Sloan McKinney were inside the jail when an explosion rocked the walls and caused the building to catch fire. Both Sheriff Matheson and Sergeant McKinney barely escaped with their lives." The camera panned across the site, capturing the destruction and violence.

"Sheriff Matheson has been taken to a safe house but continues to work in conjunction with the Texas Rangers to solve the current homicide, which appears to be connected to the murder of Lou Anne Wallace sixteen years ago."

"Do they have any leads yet?" an elderly man asked from the crowd.

A woman in the front row hugged her children to her side protectively. "When will there be an arrest?"

"Did Jim McKinney kill Sarah Wallace and her mother?" someone else shouted.

Dennison caught sight of Joey, and a predatory gleam appeared in his eyes. "Good question. I see someone here who might have the answer."

Joey braced herself for a confrontation. Dennison was like a snake coiled to attack anyone even remotely related to the crime.

And she was definitely related.

"Miss Hendricks is from the governor's office and, I believe, one of your own home-grown girls." He offered a challenging look that sent alarm bells clanging in her head. His comment had been a direct hit to irk her.

She'd heard his ugly insinuations before. As if she was unworthy of working with the esteemed governor. The daughter of a small-town drunk and a rich oil baron father who might have sold his own baby's life for a dollar.

Well, a hundred thousand to be exact, but same difference.

"Would you like to address the citizens?" Dennison extended the microphone to her as if they were working together.

Not on his life, they weren't.

But Joey had learned how to play the game with the big guns. And she'd be damned if she'd let this pigheaded moron intimidate her.

She pasted on a professional smile and accepted the mike. "Joey Hendricks here. I am a special investigator with the governor's office. I want to assure the residents that the governor is aware of the situation in Justice. The Department of Public Safety and the Texas Rangers are working diligently to solve the recent homicide as well as the murder of Lou Anne Wallace, and the attempted murders of Anna Wallace, Sheriff

Matheson and Sergeant McKinney. We intend to restore a sense of peace and order to Justice as soon as possible." She smiled, injecting confidence into each word. "It's imperative that you folks remain calm. If you have any information pertaining to these crimes, no matter how insignificant, please step forward. Together, we can end the terror seizing the town."

Dennison arched a brow. "So that means that you're prepared to own up to your family's possible involvement in the murders?"

Heat caused rivulets of perspiration to collect on her nape. "I trust the Texas Rangers and Justice Police Department to find the truth." She gestured toward the black-sooted police department building. "In spite of the recent demise of our local facility, the law enforcement agents are working 24/7. When information becomes available, I will see that it is dispensed to facilitate an arrest." She leveled a warning look at Dennison. "After all, we don't want the investigation ruined by false reporting or irresponsible press coverage."

Dennison moved like a true viper. "Is it true that the police are focusing the investigation on your parents, Miss Hendricks? That your father tampered with his own surveillance tapes to hide his part in your brother's kidnapping and murder? That he killed his wife, Lou Anne, because she intended to disclose his scheme?"

Joey's insides clenched, a tremor running through her, although she tried desperately to mask any reaction. "As I said before, I will disclose information as soon as the facts become available. To speculate about unsubstantiated allegations would be detrimental to the investigation."

He opened his mouth to continue his interrogation, but she cut him off with a withering look. "Thank you in advance for your cooperation." She shoved the microphone back in Dennison's hand and walked away.

Head high, shoulders rigid, she passed the inn, then the Main Street Diner and headed to the one spot in town that held a few precious good memories. Although there were bad ones there, as well.

The Last Call. She'd dragged her mother

from the bar more times than she could count. Had driven her home and helped her to bed, listening to her vent her anger at Leland for his infidelities and her anguish over her missing toddler son.

But Joey had had her first taste of hard liquor in the establishment, too. And lost her virginity afterward.

A sardonic laugh escaped her. Sex was out of the question tonight.

But a drink was definitely in the picture.

Something strong to help her forget that her parents were once again smack-dab in the middle of a homicide investigation. That she blamed them for her brother's disappearance.

That her own guilt was unbearable.

Suddenly a low roar rent the night air, and tires screeched. A lone headlight blared in her eyes. She froze momentarily, then realized it wasn't a car, but a motorcycle careening toward her. A Harley with a leather-clad man all in black.

His tires screeched and sparks flew from the asphalt. He obviously didn't see her.

And if she didn't move fast, he was going to plow right into her.

Chapter Two

Cole gripped the handlebars with a white-knuckled grip as he skidded sideways. Sparks flew from the asphalt, and his tires ground against the gravel, sending small rocks scattering in a dozen directions. Instead of having the good sense to move, the leggy blonde froze in place, making the blood rush to his head and sending a shard of panic through his chest.

He had to miss her, but damn—he didn't want to tear up the expensive machine below him, either.

Okay, she was much more important than his Harley, but still…

He caught the bulk of the bike's weight with his muscled strength, tilted his body sideways to compensate for the spin and to keep the Hog from rolling, then roared past her and skidded to a stop near the rail hitching post in front of the Last Call. She jumped into the shadows of the awning just as he cut the engine.

Hissing a sigh of relief and frustration, he shot off the bike, whirled around and glared at her. Adrenaline fired his veins and sent a furious round of curse words sailing past his lips. He wanted to wrap his hands around her delectable little throat. "What the…didn't your mother teach you not to stand in the street?"

"You moron!" she shouted back at the same moment. "You nearly killed me."

Moron? "*You're* questioning *my* intelligence?" He ripped off his helmet, then slung his hair out of his face. "Dammit, sugar, you're the one who needs to watch where you're going!"

"I could say the same thing to you." She jabbed a sharp red fingernail at his chest. "I don't know what kind of hole you crawled out of, but pedestrians have the right-of-way in this town, and the speed limit is…well, you were way over it."

Her scathing words reminded him too quickly what he'd already known—that he shouldn't expect a warm welcome in Justice. That some people here thought he was a low-life slime just because he was the bastard son of Jim McKinney.

The very reason he'd headed to the bar first thing.

Before he faced his half brothers the next morning, he intended to have a cold one, unwind and cool off. And where better to get the local scoop than the town's pub?

Loose lips liked to talk....

A sliver of moonlight caught her blond hair and sassy eyes, and his gut did an odd flip-flop. She was the hottest woman he'd ever laid eyes on. Her bare legs came up to her neck, the suit jacket she wore had popped the top button and a generous amount of cleavage spilled over the top of a black lacy camisole beneath. Damn.

He'd never met a drink or a woman he didn't like, or at least wanted to taste. And this was one tall drink of water that tempted his thirst, badly.

"You give every man you meet this much trouble?"

She gave him a scathing look. "Men are nothing but cheaters and liars. They use women, then walk away when they're finished."

"Ouch." She'd been hurt badly by someone. He swallowed against the sudden dryness of his throat. He felt as if he'd eaten dust. Or maybe her comment hit too close to home. "What if I said I'm sorry?"

She tossed a silky-looking strand of hair over her shoulder. "For yourself or for the sorriness of all those with the Y chromosome?"

His mouth twitched. "Both."

Her lips finally quirked. "All right. I…I…guess you're forgiven."

She glanced back at the jail cell standing like a monument in the center of town across the street, and he realized she might have just come from that media circus. She didn't look happy about it, either.

He'd sped past it, irritated at the thought of facing the mangy reporters. He imagined the headlines with a snarl.

Poor little illegitimate son shows up in town to help exonerate his father.

So what was her problem with them?

Not that he cared, but looking at her was a nice diversion. "Let me buy you a cold one. You look like you need it as much as I do."

"You can't imagine." She rolled her shoulders, and a whispery sigh escaped her that made his chest tighten.

Man, he did like women. All their softness. The way they smelled. The feel of their skin against his.

And hers looked soft and creamy. And her voice, now she'd stopped screaming at him, sounded low and throaty.

Sultry.

Oblivious to the train of his lustful thoughts, she sashayed ahead of him and reached for the door. His gaze latched on to the rounded curve of her hips in that short, tight skirt, and his hands itched to reach out and wrap themselves around her tush.

He shoved them into his pockets instead. Women were trouble, and he was here on business, not to get laid or involved with a local.

A sea of smoke and noise engulfed him as they entered the bar. Willie Nelson's voice droned out from the jukebox, peanut shells littered the scarred wooden floor, and the scent of beer and cigarette smoke clouded the room.

Ahh, pure heaven to a man's senses.

She hesitated slightly, though, and he noticed the men in the back stop their pool game to gape at her. At the same time, two old-timers sharing a pitcher turned to ogle her, and the bartender, a fortysomething bald man with a thick neck, raised an appreciative brow. This girl would not be paying for her own drinks. No sirree.

But what would the jerks expect in return?

Cole's protective instincts surged to life. "How about a booth?"

She plunked into a corner one, and he claimed the seat across from her, then shot the other men a warning look as if to say she was off-limits. Outside the shadows of night and the awning had shielded her face, but although the lights were dim now, he saw her face clearly. He'd thought he'd sweated outside in his leathers with the summer heat beating down on him on the ride into Justice, but his temperature skyrocketed toward the hundreds as he realized who this sexy bombshell was.

Joey Hendricks—he'd seen her several times on television beside the governor. Holy hell. She was a hotshot special investigator with the state.

And she was also the daughter of the oil baron Leland Hendricks, who'd been accused of the kidnapping and murder of his own child. Hendricks and his ex-wife, Donna, had been major suspects in the murder of Lou Anne Wallace.

The reason she was here hit him like a fist in his gut. She had come for the same reason he had.

Because of the Wallace homicide investigation.

And if he guessed right, her parents were probably suspects in this new murder as well as the first one.

JOEY STRUGGLED TO STEADY her breathing. Her adrenaline was still racing from the confrontation with Dennison and then nearly getting mowed down in the street. And the sight of this biker dude...wow.

All that black leather, dark black scraggly hair down to his shoulders, scruffy bearded face, sweat beading on his forehead gave him a threatening look.

But not in a way that said he might physically hurt her. In a way that screamed raw, primal sexuality. Like a man who'd just returned from a long, heated battle against a beast in the wilderness, a battle he'd no doubt won.

As he would win over any woman he met. All it took was one look into those enigmatic, brooding eyes and the sound of that husky deep voice, and she'd forgotten the fact that he'd nearly killed her.

The moron.

Then again, on closer inspection, his eyes did hold a level of intelligence. Street-smart, not all book-bred. This guy had been around and knew the ropes.

And heaven help her, that incredibly fit body conjured wicked fantasies. He had wide broad shoulders. Pecs to die for. Muscular thighs that could pin a woman beneath him while he tortured her with his tongue.

He gestured toward the bartender, and she took advantage of the moment to assess him in more detail. Even his hands were large, broad. His blunt, strong fingers were sprinkled with dark hair that made her wonder what they would fccl like on her. Touching her. Stroking her sensitive skin.

A jagged scar jutted out from the neckline of his black T-shirt, and she imagined the rest of his body beneath. A chest sprinkled with the same dark hair, another scar maybe. And a tattoo or two hidden somewhere on his bronzed skin.

What was she doing? He wasn't her type. She liked sophisticated, educated men. Men with jobs. Men who shaved and bathed regularly.

"What'll you have, sugar?" he drawled.

You. She gaped at his mouth, then realized that she was acting like a fool. And Joey Hendricks, professional investigator for the governor, was not a fool. Never had been. Not over a man.

She'd taken notes from her parents' disastrous divorce and her father's infidelities, and decided relationships just weren't worth the trouble. Although a one-nighter, especially with a hunk like this guy, might be fun. A stress release. Maybe even mind-altering. Certainly hotter than any night she'd experienced in years.

Then she remembered her reason for coming to Justice and vetoed the idea.

The drink would have to suffice. "A shot of tequila."

He arched a thick brow, and she raised her own in challenge. "What? You don't think I can handle it?"

"Honey, I think you can handle anything that comes your way."

With one flick of his hand, he waved the waitress over—a twentysomething girl who turned eyes of adoration toward him—then ordered Joey a shot and a Stella for himself.

He would order a beer with a woman's name. "You don't like tequila?" she asked.

He leaned back against the booth edge, stretched his long legs out so one of them brushed hers beneath the table. "On the contrary. José and I have been best friends for years."

She couldn't help herself. She grinned at

his statement. He looked like a tequila-drinking hellion straight from a biker's fest. She imagined him stuffing dollars into the bras of women as they bared their chests for him, and her senses hummed with awareness.

What was wrong with her?

For all she knew he might be a freeloader who had women in ten different cities, and kids to go with each one. Kids he'd never claimed.

Or he could be a criminal.

He turned his dark eyes on her just as the waitress delivered their drinks.

"Thanks." He grabbed the beer and moved the shot in front of Joey.

The girl stood beside him for a moment as if waiting for him to address her again. Annoyed when he didn't pay her more attention, she gave Joey a decidedly unfriendly stare as if they were schoolkids fighting over the only boy in town.

Pickings must be slim in Justice. She should warn the waitress to steer clear of men like him—untrustworthy men in titillating packages that screamed with sex appeal—then decided to heed the warning herself.

She didn't intend to be in Justice long. Then again, she'd have to stay until this case was solved.

And deal with her parents...

What if one of them was arrested? What if they were guilty?

Her lungs tightened at the thought, and she sprinkled salt on her hand, licked it, tossed down the shot, sucked the lime, then dropped the shot glass onto the table with a smile. As she swiped her hand across her mouth, an intense, hungry look flared in his deep-set eyes.

"You want another one, Joey?"

Her breath caught. How did he know her name?

The newscast...he must have seen it.

"In a minute. But I'm afraid you have me at a disadvantage." She straightened, reminding herself that her image counted. Especially if she intended to counteract the negative one she'd been saddled with thanks to her mother and father's tawdry actions. "You know who I am, but you haven't introduced yourself."

His cocky smile faltered slightly. As if stalling, he took a long pull of his beer, set it down and scraped his hair off his forehead. Then finally he leaned forward, his dark eyes trained on her. "Sergeant Cole McKinney, Texas Ranger."

Joey licked her lips in stunned silence.

This hot-as-all-get-out biker bad boy was Cole McKinney? The Cole McKinney, illegitimate child of Jim McKinney? The boy who'd been shunned by the McKinney family?

And he was a Texas Ranger? A law enforcement agent?

Not a freeloading biker or a criminal.

"I see the wheels turning in your head, Joey Hendricks." His husky voice skated over her raw nerve endings. "And yeah, I'm that Cole McKinney, a sum of all those rotten things you were thinking. And a few more you don't even know about."

"I...what are you doing here?" she whispered.

A bitter laugh followed, husky and filled with emotions she was certain he hadn't meant to reveal. Then quiet acceptance registered in his intense eyes as if he expected skepticism. Even disdain.

And he probably did. He'd been an outcast from the town all his life.

"Believe it nor not," he said quietly, "the Texas Rangers requested my services as a tracker to help find Sarah Wallace's killer."

Suddenly at a loss for words, she didn't protest when Cole raised his hand and ordered her another shot. Instead she accepted it graciously, then studied him with a different eye. If the Texas Rangers had requested his assistance, he must be damn good at his job.

What did he know about the investigation? Something the Rangers hadn't revealed to the press?

Her hand trembled as she turned up the second shot glass.

Was he here to arrest one or both of her parents?

COLE TOOK ANOTHER long pull of the beer, hoping the cold liquid would chill the fire burning his body. A heat caused both from his temper at her reaction to his name and his body reacting with lust to her every movement.

"So, Cole, how did you get to be a Ranger?"

A smile quirked his mouth. If he didn't know better, he'd think he'd just made the woman nervous.

Then again, knowing what he did about her family, he figured the Rangers were probably the last people she wanted to see.

And his brothers probably would resent her interference, as well. Since the Rangers were part of the state agency, they'd think the governor sent her to spy on them. Hell, he probably had.

"I joined the Army at seventeen," he said with a shrug. Unlike Zane, who'd gone to college, earned a degree in criminal justice and worked in criminal investigation. Or Sloan, who had been sheriff of Justice.

"Then I spent some time in the Middle East, got into military security." Sniper training to be exact, but he didn't have to spill his guts. Like how many kills he had under his belt. "When I got out, I joined the DPS and became a motorcycle state trooper for a couple of years."

She cocked a brow at that, and he grinned. "The way you handled that bike, you must have grown up on a Harley."

He laughed, then sobered as he remembered how hard he'd worked to earn his first bike. Just the way he'd scraped for everything in his life. "Naw, on a ranch, but I was a bull rider." And he wanted to ride her.

The thought made him tighten his fingers around the long neck of the beer bottle. He could not get involved with Joey Hendricks. Even though he'd earned the college credits necessary for the Rangers, he was rough around the edges. He'd hunted down the worst dregs of society, worked undercover in operations that would make her head spin. He'd killed and not looked back.

She was sophisticated. Educated. Out of his league.

And although she worked for the governor and might not admit it, she was tied to this town and her family. Had a vested interest in protecting her parents, whereas he was tied to no one. Didn't care who was arrested as long as justice was served. In fact, he wouldn't be in town long enough to let the dust settle on his seat. And if he had to lock up one of his blood kin, so be it.

"So, you haven't seen your brothers yet?" she asked.

"You mean half brothers?" He finished his beer, then grunted. "Nope. I'll have that pleasure in the morning."

She nodded, and drummed her fingernails on the table, then glanced around the bar, looking restless again. Or was she looking for someone in particular?

"What about you? Visited your family yet?"

Pain tightened her features. "No. Haven't spoken to Mommy and Daddy dearest in years."

Now, that surprised him. On second thought, he didn't know why. From what he'd read about the homicide investigation into the case of Lou Anne Wallace, about Joey's brother's kidnapping and her mother's past drinking problem, her family was as dysfunctional as the McKinneys. But still, family ties ran thick and deep.

Was she here in an official capacity, or had she come because of her own secret agenda—to see that her mother and father weren't arrested for the crimes?

Chapter Three

Cole finally dragged his butt into the shower at dawn. He hadn't slept worth a flip for thinking about the investigation and wondering how his brothers would react to the sight of him. Not that he cared…

And then there had been the fantasies about a certain sexpot blonde that had plagued him all night long.

After their drink, he'd walked her to the inn where they both were staying. Adding more fuel to the flames of his imagination, he learned she was in the room right next door to him, so they'd shared an awkward but titillating moment in the hallway as they'd said good night. Awkward because he'd damn near forgotten his head and kissed her. Titillating because he'd sensed she'd wanted it as much as he had, and that she would have let him.

Then they would have ended up in bed for some mind-blowing sex—at least that's where the kiss had led in his fertile fantasy—and he would have at least felt sated, if not rested.

Now he just felt irritable and restless.

Because nothing had happened.

He showered and managed to find a razor, wishing he'd had time for a haircut, then cursed himself for worrying about his appearance. He didn't give a damn what his brothers thought—or anyone else in town.

Grimacing, he dressed in his normal Ranger wear: clean jeans, a white Western shirt, boots, belt and tie. Determined to prove he was a top-notch Ranger himself, he pinned on his badge and grabbed his Stetson and the folder of notes he had collected on the first investigation of Lou Anne Wallace's murder sixteen years ago. Then he headed to that diner he'd seen last night, to pick up some breakfast before he met the McKinney brothers and the local deputies for a briefing. If he was here to track evidence in the woods, he needed food and coffee, and lots of it.

After all, he had a big advantage over his half brothers. He wasn't personally attached to Jim McKinney or anyone else in town.

A BLOODCURDLING SCREAM pierced the air and forced thirteen-year-old Joey from her peaceful sleep.

Her mother.

She threw the covers aside, jumped up and ran to the door. But when she swung it open, a thick plume of smoke curled through the hallway. The scent of charred wood and fabric hit her. Oh God, the house was on fire!

Her father…no, daddy was at his house.

She had to get to her mother…but where was she?

And little Justin?

His room was downstairs next to her mother's.

Joey ran through the fog of smoke, feeling for the banister to help guide her, coughing and choking as she made her way to the door of the nursery. Flames licked the walls in the kitchen and crawled along the floor in the den. The curtains erupted into a ball of fire and sparks flew from the ceiling. Wood crackled and popped, splintering as the table collapsed into flames.

Her mother was already awake, standing at the crib.

Joey's eyes stung from the smoke. "We have to get out of here!"

Her mother spun around, eyes wild with terror, a crazed expression on her face. "Where's my baby? What did you do with him? You were supposed to watch him for me!"

Joey's heart pounded as she rushed forward to check the crib. Little Justin was not inside. Panic stabbed at her chest, robbing her of air. Where was her baby brother? Had he crawled out? Could he be somewhere in the house?

No, please no, the fire…it might have gotten him already. Or he might have inhaled too much smoke…

Her mother jerked her by her pajama shirt and shook her. "Where is he, Joey? Where's my baby? What did you do with him?"

"*Mom! I don't know. Let me go.*" *She yanked her mother's fingers away.* "*I'll look for him.*"

The scent of liquor permeated her mother's breath. "*Tell me what you did with him!*"

Joey's heart wrenched. "*I put him to bed...he was here.*" *A sob racked her, and heat scalded her face. The fire was slipping toward the hall. They had to get out.*

"*Please, Mom, call the fire department. I'll hunt for Justin!*"

Her mother threw her hands in the air. "*No! He's gone—he's not here! Someone took him, I know it!*"

"*Mother, call the fire department. We need help! And get Rosa!*" *Joey frantically searched the room and closet to see if Justin might have hidden inside. But no Justin.*

Outside, a siren wailed, indicating that someone had phoned the firemen. Probably Rosa. Thank heavens. Now, if she could just find her little brother...

But she couldn't search with her mother in hysterics, so she dragged her into the hallway. The kitchen was engulfed in flames. She couldn't go that way. The front door was smoky, the flames licking at the wall casing and rippling a path of fire in front of it. Her heart racing, she glanced around the room for her baby brother, but didn't see him. Maybe he was in the playroom upstairs.

Suddenly Rosa raced into the hallway, a stricken look on her face. "Hurry! Out the window in my room!"

"We can't, we have to find Justin!" Joey screamed. "Take Mom outside. I'll look for him!"

She shoved her mother toward Rosa, and her mother crumbled in Rosa's arms. Joey lurched toward the steps to search upstairs, but firemen crashed through the front, spraying water. Chaos erupted. One of the firemen grabbed Rosa and her mother, and another one ran toward her.

"Come on, this house is going down!" he yelled. "You can't go upstairs! No time to save your things!"

"My baby brother...we can't find him!" Joey cried.

The fireman gently coaxed her toward the other man. "Get out of here now! We'll find the boy!"

JOEY JERKED AWAKE and sat up, sweating and shaking. Tears rained down her face, the familiar guilt and terror gripping her full force.

The chaos. The firemen hacking away the window, breaking glass. Pushing her mother, Rosa, then her outside. Them collapsing on the lawn and watching in abject shock as the flames engulfed room after room and the house collapsed in front of them.

The firemen eventually appearing through the haze of smoke and debris, looking dazed, frustrated, sorrowful.

Their arms empty. They hadn't found Justin.

Then her father had driven up, frantic and acting like a madman as he discovered the horror.

For the next forty-eight hours, she and her mother had moved on autopilot. Her mother had had to be sedated. Her father had stalked the police for a report.

Joey had blamed herself. And in every waking or sleeping moment she'd heard her little brother's cry.

Then finally a small amount of relief.

The reports proved that Justin had not been in the fire.

He had disappeared instead.

The theory was that he'd been kidnapped. The fire had been a ruse to distract them.

And then a new kind of terror had seized them. Fear that a monster had Justin. A sexual predator. A child killer. They'd imagined the worst. And then the horrible wait. Hoping and praying for a phone call. A ransom note.

But the note and call had never come.

Which had made them all suspect that something had gone wrong with the kidnapping.

And that Justin was dead after all.

The nightmare had magnified tenfold after that. The police had turned on the family. Questioned them all. Donna. Her father. Even Joey and Rosa.

And eventually they'd accused her father of planning the kidnapping/murder for the insurance money.

Joey swiped tears from her eyes and headed to the shower. Although it had been sixteen years since that day, she still smelled the smoke and sweat on her skin. Still felt the flames singeing her skin, heard her mother's cries of terror and the accusations she'd hurled. And the image of her father breaking down had been etched in her mind.

Had his tears been real? Or had he planned the disappearance of her brother and his grief had been an act?

Had her brother not disappeared, would her parents ever have reconciled? Not with Lou Anne in the picture...

The very motive the police had attached to her mother years ago.

Donna had cloaked herself in bitterness after the divorce. Mentally Joey recognized the fact that the problems between her parents had driven the family apart long before the kidnapping/murder. But Justin's disappearance had ended any chance they'd had of reclaiming a normal, civilized relationship.

She would never be free of the guilt.

Her stomach twisted into a knot. She was here to help find the answers.

But heaven help her, she was afraid of what the grand jury might find.

IT HADN'T OCCURRED TO COLE when he'd entered the café that the owner of the Main Street Diner was Joey's mother. But with her flaming red hair, he'd recognized her instantly from old news photos. Dressed in an immaculate pantsuit with pearls around her neck, she greeted the customers while an Hispanic woman she called Rosa bustled around filling coffee mugs and serving breakfast.

Donna had given him the once-over when he'd first entered, as if she thought she should recognize him but didn't. And she'd glanced at him with hooded eyes a dozen times since, trying to figure him out.

He hadn't offered up his identity. Right now his anonymity might play in his favor.

"More coffee?" Rosa asked.

He nodded and thanked her for topping up his cup. "Those biscuits were the best I've ever tasted."

"Gracias, señor." She strode away with a smile of pride, although when she joined Donna, they disappeared into the back room speaking in hushed voices.

He reread the notes on the kidnapping/

murder investigation while he polished off his steak and eggs. Donna Hendricks's drinking problem, coupled with her husband's affairs, had led to a bitter divorce and custody battle. Both Joey, thirteen at the time, and Donna's toddler son, Justin, were caught in the war, but Leland had won custody. Then one night, when Joey and Justin were at Donna's, a horrible fire had broken out. Rosa Ramirez had been the care-taker/nanny and housekeeper for Donna when Justin had been kidnapped.

Cole had been a teenager himself, but news of the fire and kidnapping/murder of the toddler had been all over TV.

In the police reports, he skimmed Donna's statement. Then Leland's. Donna had been despondent over her son's disappearance and the possibility of his death. She'd nearly had a breakdown and had been treated for de-pression. Leland had appeared to be dis-traught, had vowed to find his son and pay for his return, no matter the cost. Both had vehemently denied allegations that they were involved in a kidnapping/murder scheme.

Joey's interview had been the tale of a

traumatized teenager. A kid who'd tried to save her drunken mother and find her baby brother in the midst of a blazing fire. A kid who probably still had nightmares of that night.

Then the speculations had started. Leland, the big oil baron, had been broke. He'd allegedly concocted a fake kidnapping/murder in order to collect on a life insurance policy. Donna had testified against her ex.

Leland had blamed Donna, and claimed that if she'd been sober, she might have heard someone break in and take their toddler.

They'd waited on a ransom note, one that hadn't arrived. The police had grown suspicious, then finally they'd decided the fake kidnapping/murder had turned sour.

More details on the family dynamics had been disclosed. Lou Anne Wallace, Leland's second wife, had been spoiled and supposedly married Leland for his money. She had her own kids, Anna and Sarah, and didn't want custody of Joey or Justin. She especially hadn't wanted a screaming two-year-old. And she'd never given up her affairs.

Cole grimaced. He imagined how miserable Joey must have felt, then clenched his jaw—he had to stop thinking about Joey Hendricks.

But her mother, Donna, was another story. She'd hated Lou Anne Wallace for marrying Leland. Donna had speculated that since Lou Anne hadn't wanted the kids around, she had helped Leland with his scheme. Others suspected Leland murdered Lou Anne because she intended to go to the police about his illegal plan.

But no one knew the truth.

Then Sarah Wallace had come to town a few days ago, supposedly with new evidence, but she'd been murdered before revealing the details.

All roads led back to the kidnapping/murder of Justin Hendricks. If they found out the truth about that night, they'd find the answers to the Wallace women's murders.

The door creaked open, and he froze with his coffee cup midway to his mouth as Joey walked in. She looked gorgeous and sexy as hell. Her long blond hair was pulled back in a clip at her nape, and she wore jeans that outlined those long legs and her tight butt, and a soft, feminine blouse that gaped above her cleavage. His mouth watered.

Last night she had admitted she hadn't spoken to her parents in years. He wondered what kind of fireworks would fly this morning between her and Donna.

What exactly did Donna Hendricks know about her son's disappearance and the murders of the Wallace women?

JOEY HAD BRACED herself to see her mother, but the sight of Donna holding a coffeepot, looking so domestic, nearly bowled her over.

She didn't know this woman at all.

Her mother had been a sloppy drunk. Joey had rescued her from brawls, helped her stagger inside the house when she'd passed out on the lawn, cleaned up her messes and put her to bed.

She'd also dragged her away from the nasty fights with her father, Donna screaming that her father was a lying, cheating bastard, Leland shouting back that Donna was a drunken whore.

Her mother glanced up at the door, then saw her and visibly paled.

Joey's throat constricted. What had she expected? For her mother to race toward her with open arms and a welcoming hug? For forgiveness for not taking better care of Justin? For the unconditional love she'd never offered?

The room grew quiet, tension vibrating through the diner that smelled of hot sausages, coffee and cinnamon rolls. Her stomach roiled. Steeling herself against the small-town gossip and whispers, she glanced across the room, searching. For what she didn't know. A familiar face? An old friend?

Not that she had any here.

Then she spotted Cole McKinney. In a sea of strangers, he looked like the least vicious of the sharks.

Heaven help her, but she headed straight for his table. Her legs felt shaky, and she clutched the table edge, then slid into the chair across from him without waiting for an invitation. He cocked one dark brow, then offered her a sideways smile of understanding. Her heart fluttered wildly, and she felt like kissing him.

Ridiculous.

Then again, she'd struggled with that same feeling the night before. A temptation she had resisted.

For good reason, too. She had no time for a fling or romantic entanglement, especially with Cole McKinney.

Although the first part of the night she'd spent fantasizing about what might have happened if she had relented. One hot kiss would have led to another. Then tawdry, naked, wild sex.

"Good mornin'," he said in a sexy drawl.

Was it? She wanted to growl. She'd heard him next door tossing and turning and pacing the floor the night before, as well.

She had to inform the Mathesons that the inn walls needed better insulation against the noise.

She nodded anyway, though, unable to speak. Her voice was lost somewhere in between fantasies of Cole, the tremors remaining from her nightmare this morning and the stunned look on her mother's face.

Donna slowly walked toward her.

Joey swallowed, then noticed the files that Cole shoved into a folder. Files about the murders. Files about her missing brother. An old photo of her and her parents at the police station being questioned after Justin's disappearance.

His solemn look told her he understood her discomfort.

He had no idea. She was behaving irrationally. Running to him as if he was her friend. As if he could save her from herself and her family when he'd come here to investigate every last one of them.

Cole McKinney had no real connections to the town or her family. If he found any dirty secrets hiding in the closet, he would have no qualms about exposing them.

No, he wasn't her friend. Couldn't help her.

No one could.

Chapter Four

Donna Hendricks's heels clicked ominously in the sudden stillness of the room. Cole watched, scrutinizing every movement. The other patrons craned their necks and their conversations quieted. Apparently they were as interested in the unfolding drama between mother and daughter as he was.

Although Joey tried to camouflage her nervous reaction, her breath rattled in the quiet tension as Donna paused beside the table.

"Joey…when did you get to town?"

Joey turned a steady, unemotional gaze on her mother. "Last night."

Donna placed a coffee mug on the table, filled it for her daughter and glanced at Cole in question as if to ask if they were together. "Where are you staying?"

"I reserved a room at the Matheson Inn."

Donna wet her ruby-red lips with her tongue. "And who's your friend here?"

A small smile curved Joey's mouth as if she was taking some perverse pleasure in watching her mother squirm. Or maybe in being seen with him in a town that lived for the rumor mill.

"This is Cole McKinney," Joey said. "*Sergeant* Cole McKinney, Texas Rangers."

Donna's mouth widened into a shocked O, then she narrowed her penciled eyebrows. "You're Jim McKinney's *other* son?"

Cole gritted his teeth at her condescending tone and gave a clipped nod. He would never call the man his father.

Donna pressed a shaky hand to her throat. "Then you're here about the investigation into Sarah Wallace's murder?"

"Yes, ma'am."

Donna angled her head toward her daughter. "And what about you, Joey? Did you come to see me or your father?"

Joey cradled the coffee mug between her hands. "The governor sent me to oversee the case, and handle the media."

Disappointment mingled with some other troubled emotion on Donna's face. Pain? Guilt? Fear of being exposed? "I see. Have you talked to Leland yet?"

Joey's look turned more strained. "No, but I'm sure I will. The Rangers will undoubtedly question him again. And I plan to sit in on all the interrogations."

Donna studied her daughter for a full minute without a reply. Then as if disappointed in Joey's comment, she gestured toward the menu. "Rosa will come and take your order."

With a blistering look, she strode back to the breakfast counter, then disappeared behind the doors leading to the back. Rosa frowned and rushed toward Joey, although when she reached the table, she hesitated as if she wasn't sure how Joey would accept her overture.

But Joey stood, sporting the first sincere smile he'd seen on her face. "Rosa...it's nice to see you."

Sadness tinged Rosa's eyes as she hugged Joey.

"Let me get you some breakfast." Rosa

patted Joey's shoulder like a doting mother. "How about one of Rosa's famous Mexican omelets, the ones you loved when you were a little *niña, sí?*"

Joey shook her head. "No, thanks, Rosa. I…don't have time."

Cole removed some bills from his wallet and laid them on the table, uncomfortable with the private moment. Time to meet his brothers and get to work. "I have to go now. Breakfast was great, Rosa."

She nodded and whispered, *"Gracias, señor."* But her dark eyes also reflected a wariness that made him wonder if she was hiding something, as well.

He would find out sooner or later. A second later Joey caught up with him. "You're on your way to the briefing?"

"Yes."

"I'm going with you. I need to catch up on the details of the investigation."

He frowned, held the door open for her, and they walked across the street to the courthouse in silence. As soon as they entered the conference room, which had been designated as a temporary office for the sheriff, the room quieted. Zane occupied the chair behind the desk as if he'd self-appointed himself head of command while Sloan was propped on the edge, looking like a relaxed hometown boy. A deputy stood by the window staring outside as if he'd been watching for Cole to warn his half brothers of his arrival.

Cole had seen pictures of both of them in the paper, had kept abreast of their careers, their commendations and awards. Both had been popular in high school. Zane, the valedictorian, Mr. JHS—Justice High School—and a quarterback on the football team. And Sloan had been a baseball star and won the state championship. They'd also been noted for their work in solving various high-profile cases.

But he had never met them face-to-face.

He was surprised at the way his stomach clenched. Both men resembled Jim to a degree, although there were subtle differences.

Judging from their solemn expressions they weren't happy about meeting him. Fine, he was a necessary evil. Here to do a job, not make friends with his siblings.

Zane gave him a clipped nod of acknowledgment. "Glad you finally made it."

Sloan's look wasn't as hospitable. "We've been waiting."

Cole returned their greeting with a scowl. Then Joey entered the room, and the tension intensified to a deafening roar.

"What the hell is she doing here?" Zane asked.

Cole wasn't surprised at their reaction.

Next to him, the last thing the Rangers wanted was a special investigator for the governor—and the daughter of a prime suspect—breathing down their necks as if the governor didn't trust them to do their jobs.

But the governor obviously recognized that each of the participants had a personal interest in the outcome of the case. His half brothers and Joey included.

And the verdict was still out over whether or not any of them were on the same side.

JOEY PLASTERED her professional, detached face in place. No doubt her position here threw a kink in their family-run operations.

The fact that she'd arrived with their illegitimate half brother hadn't ingratiated her with the McKinney men, either.

But she refused to let these men intimidate her with their macho, own-the-town attitudes. She'd told the governor the McKinneys wouldn't welcome her nosing into what they considered *their* investigation, but the case had drawn statewide attention, and the Rangers investigating one of their own, especially their father, meant lines could be crossed.

She smiled smoothly and claimed a seat at the conference table with the local deputies. "You know why I'm here. You're too close to the people involved."

"And you're not?" Zane said sarcastically.

She shrugged. "My parents and I aren't exactly tight. Besides, I'm a professional. The governor wants this case solved, and he's the boss."

"We're professionals, too, and can handle the case just fine without you," Zane said.

Joey folded her hands in front of her on the table. "Listen, I'm not going home until we've ended this investigation and someone is arrested for Sarah Wallace's murder. So you'll have to put up with me, boys." She gave them a saccharine grin. "Besides, look on the bright side. I can run interference with the media. You don't want a circus in town creating panic and trying your suspects before you make an arrest."

Cole claimed the chair beside her, enjoying her spunky side. "All right, now that our happy little party is assembled, why don't you fill us in on what you have so far? If I'm tracking in the woods today, I'd like to get started."

Zane huffed and Sloan made a disgusted sound, but gestured toward the whiteboard on the wall, which held various facts, including the TOD for Lou Anne's and Sarah Wallace's murders.

"All right," Zane began. "Sarah Wallace came to town to meet her sister, Anna, and share evidence she'd uncovered about their mother's death. She used a prepaid cell phone, which we haven't recovered yet, to phone Anna, but when Anna arrived, she found Sarah's body in the hotel room. She was already dead, had been strangled like her mother. Later someone tried to kill Anna in the same way."

"Why kill Anna?" Joey asked.

"Apparently the killer thought Anna knew something to incriminate him. Or her."

Cole nodded. "Did she?"

"No. But later, Anna remembered a false bottom in one of their mother's suitcases. Sarah had it with her," Zane explained. "We examined it and found papers Sarah had hidden inside. The notes and papers indicated that Donna Hendricks might have intended to pay off Lou Anne for providing her with information about Leland's alleged plans to fake the kidnapping and murder of his son. We're getting a search warrant now to access Donna's financial records, along with Rosa's."

"So you believe Lou Anne blackmailed Donna?" Cole asked.

Sloan nodded. "Lou Anne didn't want more kids, so when she discovered Leland's plan, she phoned Donna to tell her. She tried to blackmail Donna into paying her for the tip. We think Donna probably agreed, but Donna wanted Lou Anne to report Leland to the FBI."

"Why wouldn't Donna just go to the police herself?" Cole asked.

"Because she was bitter over losing the custody battle," Sloan supplied. "Without evidence, Leland could have accused her of conspiring with him to pull off the kidnapping/murder. Or he could have accused her of orchestrating the entire plan herself and she'd lose any visitation rights with her children."

"And no one would believe my mother because she was a drunk back then." Joey understood the implied assumption. It was possible that when Lou Anne refused to go to the FBI, Donna had killed her.

"What about Rosa?" Joey drummed her nails on the table. "Why are you looking at her records?"

"She bought liquor and drugs for Donna," Zane interjected. "If Donna wanted to hide money to pay off a blackmailer, she might have enlisted Rosa's help."

"Has Donna confessed to any of this?" Cole asked.

Zane grimaced. "No, not yet."

"While Zane's been handling the grand jury, I stepped in to help Sheriff Matheson,"

Sloan said. "We were studying the papers Sarah left when the fire broke out in the jail. Then someone tried to shoot Carley." Anger hardened Sloan's face. "She's in a safe house now, but she's searching Donna's financial records for more details."

"So you're focusing on my parents now?" Joey asked. Could one of them be a murderer? Had her mother or father killed Lou Anne, and now Sarah? Had one of them really shot the sheriff to keep her from finding out the truth?

Her stomach knotted again. "I thought Leland had an alibi for the night of Lou Anne's murder?"

Zane's boots hit the floor with a thud. "We discovered that he tampered with the surveillance cameras, so his alibi is shot."

"What about your father, Jim McKinney?" Joey asked. "He was seen leaving the inn that night."

The men traded an odd look.

"What are you not saying?" Cole asked.

Sloan twisted sideways and Zane clenched his jaw. "We haven't ruled out Jim yet."

"And Stella?" Joey asked. "She hated Lou Anne for her affair with Jim."

Pain flashed into both men's eyes. "Stella had a breakdown," Zane said. "She's in the hospital, despondent. I'm not sure how much more information we'll get from her."

"Dad…" Sloan paused, then continued, "Jim agreed to see a psychiatrist to try to jog his memory of the events of that night, but Stella got upset and told him no. Then she broke down. The stress has been unbearable for her."

"She was always fragile," Zane said in a low voice.

Joey frowned and steepled her hands. They seemed completely focused on making her parents out to be the villains. And Zane and Sloan were keeping secrets. Something about Stella and their father.

Her cell phone rang, and she checked the number. Governor Grange.

"Excuse me, guys. I have to take this." She stepped away from them and answered the call.

"Joey, how's it going in Justice?"

"The Rangers are conferencing now," Joey said. "No definitive leads yet. They've brought in Sergeant Cole McKinney to track evidence in the woods near the inn."

A long sigh filled with tension followed. "I hope they tie this up soon and put the guy responsible for these murders away. How is Dennison?"

"I can handle him," Joey said.

"Good. Keep me posted."

Joey agreed and pocketed her phone, contemplating Zane's and Sloan's summary of the investigation.

What were the McKinney brothers hiding?

If her parents were guilty…well, she'd have to find a way to accept it. But if they were innocent, she didn't want them railroaded to jail for a crime they hadn't committed. After all, they had suffered terribly over Justin's death.

Perhaps Stella had suffered a breakdown out of guilt. Maybe she had killed Lou Anne and had hidden behind a weak woman's facade all these years to deflect suspicion from herself.

COLE TRIED TO IGNORE the quick flash of worry in Joey's eyes. He'd just met the woman. He could not let himself care about her or how the outcome of this investigation might affect her personally.

"So, what exactly am I looking for?" Cole asked.

"We need an expert to search the woods by the inn," Sloan said. "The night Sarah Wallace was murdered, Sheriff Matheson saw a figure in dark clothing. She chased the culprit into the woods, but he shot her in the ribs. Actually cracked one. We'd like to recover any bullet casing or other evidence that you might find."

Cole stood. "I assume you have a horse available, along with the standard crime scene kit and supplies."

Zane stood, as well. "At your disposal."

"Meanwhile, I'm going to get that search warrant for Donna's records," Sloan said.

Cole nodded, anxious to get outside. He loved the fresh air, the scents of nature, the sunshine beating on his face. Fieldwork was his specialty, not digging through files, although he did plenty of that, too.

Twenty minutes later, he saddled a beautiful quarter horse named Apache, strapped on the supplies he'd need in the saddlebags and rode into the woods. Sloan and Zane had searched the edge, so he needed to go deeper. Find out how the killer had escaped. Locate that bullet.

Although it had rained recently, and some evidence might have washed away, he slowed Apache to a walk and studied each section of the forest, each patch of weeds and each tree for signs that someone had recently been through. A broken branch. Trampled bramble. An indentation in the bark not made by an animal. Each detail provided a clue and indicated he was on the right track.

He noticed a footpath along with muddy prints, although dead leaves and debris created problems in lifting a print. Still, he tied Apache to a tree and combed the area on foot, kneeling to inspect the markings and the ground. He photographed each patchy section and collected dirt for trace in hopes that they might be able to match it to a suspect's shoes and make an arrest.

Working diligently, he took a partial molding of the footprint, as well. It would give them a general clue as to the size of their suspect. A fiber from a piece of clothing was caught in a branch, and he removed an evidence bag and tweezers, snagged the fiber and bagged it to send to forensics. The next few hours he combed each mile of the woods, then finally traced his way back toward the inn and his horse. He found two other fibers, along with more footprints— muddied and misshapen, different from the first ones—so he took the best print he could lift.

Not for the first time, he considered the fact that they might be dealing with more than one perp here. What if the killer had an accomplice? Donna and Leland could have worked together. Or one of them could have hired help to do their dirty work.

About seventy-five feet to the right of where he'd tied Apache, he noticed a shattered piece of bark on a live oak. He removed the magnifying glass from his bag and examined it, then decided a bullet had scraped past. He collected the sample, bagged it, then turned and assessed the area. The bullet had grazed Carley, then bounced off the tree, which had slowed its descent. Noting the location where Sloan said the sheriff had been running, and had been shot, he estimated the trajectory of the bullet and where the shooter might have been standing when he'd fired. Zeroing in on the angle, he calculated the speed and scrutinized the other foliage until he located the shell. With gloved fingers, he picked it up and studied it. A .38.

Hell, half the town probably owned guns, and half of those were probably .38s. But modern science could do wonders. If they had a suspect and his gun, they would be able to match it.

He searched for other bullets and evidence, but found nothing. A few feet away, though, something shiny glinted through a patch of bramble. Sweat beaded on his forehead and trickled down his neck as he recognized the item.

The silver star of Texas—a Ranger's badge.

The badges were handmade from Mexican silver coins, making each one unique, and easily identifiable to its recipient. Some badges still had coin lines on the outer rim of the circle, and you could see the peso on the back of the badge. The coin on the back wasn't always at a perfect upright angle, either, and had distortions caused from being handmade.

He swallowed against the sudden dryness in his throat as he lifted it to the sun. When Jim McKinney's badge had been reported missing years ago, right after Lou Anne Wallace's murder, a description had been posted. The badge had three coin marks on the lower right star point.

He flipped the badge over and grimaced as he scrutinized the point.

If he was right, this star had belonged to Jim McKinney, his bastard father. According to police reports, Jim had claimed he'd lost it the night Lou Anne Wallace was murdered.

Chapter Five

Joey rubbed her temple where a headache throbbed. There had been enough charged electricity in that meeting between the McKinney brothers to start a brushfire. Outside, she breathed in the fresh air, hoping to calm her nerves, but she spotted her mother approaching and her anxiety rose another notch. The reporter from hell, Harold Dennison, trailed behind her like a fox chasing a rabbit.

Which one would be the lesser of two evils?

"Joey, please wait. I'd like to talk to you," Donna called.

Joey halted, knowing the confrontation was inevitable. Besides, she'd be lying to herself if she said she'd come here only because of the governor's request. She was secretly afraid the grand jury would indict one or both of her parents, and she wanted answers. Running wouldn't help her get to the truth.

Donna's eyes flitted nervously across the street, then behind Joey. Instantly recognizing the press, she stopped and her mouth flattened into a thin line. "Let's step into my office so we can talk in private."

Joey nodded, her shoulders tense as she followed Donna through the back door of the restaurant and into an office. She was surprised by the minimalist furnishings. Simple oak desk, leather chair, a love seat in the corner beside a potted plant. The room almost looked homey. Much more domestic than the mother she remembered.

Still, Donna didn't have a hair out of place. Joey felt like an awkward teenager beside her with her linen pantsuit, manicured nails and skillfully applied makeup.

In fact, she'd never quite fitted the mold of what her parents envisioned as the perfect daughter. Donna would have liked a petite ballerina or cheerleader. Leland had wanted a boy—the reason he'd nicknamed her Joey instead of Josie or called her by her full name. Then he'd had Justin, and for a while she'd thought he might be happy.

But her mother's drinking and her father's financial problems had torn them apart. Then came the nightmare of the custody battle, her brother's disappearance and the allegations against her father.

Joey had felt betrayed by them all. And what about Justin? Had he died when he was two? Where had the killer left his small body? It had never been recovered. The image of his trusting cherub face still haunted her.

And what if he was still alive? If so, where had he been all these years? Had a family adopted him? Did he remember that he had a big sister?

Even that hope was tainted with worry, though. If he had survived, someone abusive, even a deviant child molester, might have taken him in. Or he could have been sold into slavery of some kind or taken across the border. He might not even know his real name.

The harsh possibilities threatened to consume her, but oblivious to her daughter's pain as always, Donna turned and smiled. "It's so good to see you, Josephine."

Joey braced herself. "Is it, Mother? I didn't think you really cared."

Donna gasped, then forced another tight smile on her face, recovering quickly. "Yes, it is. I realize that the last time we saw each other things were unpleasant. But I've changed, sweetheart. I don't drink anymore."

Joey twined her fingers together.

"And I've no need for pills, either, so you see, I'm clean. I have been for a long time." She gestured around the office. "This is my life. The business, this café. It may not seem like much to you now that you work for the governor, but it's mine and I'm proud of it."

Sincerity and wariness underscored Donna's words, at odds with the bitterness that Donna wore as a second skin. "That's good, Mother. I'm glad to see you're…happy now."

Her mother's false smile faded slightly. "Well, that happiness and peace may not last.

Not if the sheriff and those McKinney men keep nosing around."

"A woman was murdered, Mother," Joey pointed out. "They have to investigate her death. You don't want a killer running free here in town again, do you?"

Donna's face paled, and she glanced down at her hands. "No, but neither do I want my name dragged through the mud." She gave Joey an imploring look. "It's taken years for me to recover from your father's...behavior, and the shame. And now those Rangers want to dredge up the past. All the painful memories of losing your brother."

Joey winced. Her mother had suffered—they all had.

"You have power now, Joey," Donna continued. "You have to convince them to stop looking into your brother's old case."

Joey's blood ran cold. Donna knew she was in charge of the press, that she was working on the investigation. Would Donna use her to find out what the police had on her?

"And why should I do that, Mother?" Joey sighed. "I'd think you of all people would want to know the truth about what happened to Justin." God knew, *she* did.

Donna glanced sideways, an odd look on her face, and Joey saw her gaze land on a photograph on the desk.

A brass frame held a picture of her and Justin standing beside the Christmas tree the holiday before he'd been abducted. The warm memory washed over Joey in a wave of nostalgia. Justin had been awestruck by the shiny twinkling lights, had babbled that he wanted a red fire truck for Christmas, and a train set and a pony. She had lifted him on her shoulders to help him hang his stocking on the mantel. She remembered his gleeful cry the next morning when he'd found the toys beneath the tree. And the Shetland pony out in the backyard...

"There's not a day that goes by that I don't think about Justin and wish we had him back," Donna said in a thick voice. She hitched in a breath, then resolve hardened her tone. "But opening up old wounds will do nothing but tear us apart again, Joey. Please, do what you can to get those Rangers off our backs. We barely survived the first time. I'm not sure any of us can live through a second go around."

Joey studied her mother's intense expression with unease. Was her mother's grief the real reason she didn't want the Rangers probing into the kidnapping/murder now? Or was it because she and Leland had gotten away scot-free years ago, and she was afraid they'd find evidence to convict them? If they did, would she expect Joey to cover for them?

LELAND HENDRICKS had been shocked the night before when he'd seen Joey on the TV with that slimeball reporter Dennison, and disappointed that she hadn't shown up at his house later that evening.

Emotions pummeled him as he watched her exit Donna's diner. Anger. Hurt. Betrayal. And a deep disappointment that she had chosen to see her mother before him.

Donna was probably gloating right now.

Then again, Joey hadn't spoken to him in years, so what did he expect?

That she'd realize he wasn't the villain everyone had painted him to be? That even though he had made terrible mistakes years ago—marrying Donna for one, marrying Lou Anne for another—that he had suffered every day since?

Dammit, he had provided a home for her when her mother had been too drunk and incapacitated on pills to stand upright. And in spite of the allegations against him, he had loved her and had never wanted Justin harmed.

Guilt weighed heavily on his soul as he headed toward the back of the diner. The past rose from the shadows like a dragon breathing a fiery trail down his neck. His life had been such a mess back then. His finances in ruins. His responsibilities to his business a pressure cooker ready to explode, problems attacking him from all sides. Then his family troubles. Donna's insatiable drinking and the drugs. And then Lou Anne—the woman had turned into a minefield of trouble herself. She hadn't been able to give up her lovers. Jim McKinney for one. She'd practically flaunted her affairs in his face. And she hadn't wanted his kids. Not Joey or Justin.

Especially not Justin.

He had to talk to Donna. Find out what new lies she might have planted in Joey's head.

A ripple of anxiety clawed at his throat. All these years Joey had hated him. He had to wonder why.

Did Joey know more about Justin's disappearance than she'd admitted?

Something that would make him look guilty?

LATE AFTERNOON shadows slanted across the land as Cole rode Apache up to the stables. Zane and Sloan stood by an official Rangers's car waiting for him as if they'd been there for hours. He tightened his jaw, glad he'd found some evidence to prove his worth, but also irritated that they hadn't waited at the makeshift sheriff's office for him. Didn't they trust him to keep the evidence intact?

He pulled on the reins and slowed Apache to a walk, patting his side and mumbling his thanks to the horse as the beast loped into the fenced corral and headed for a drink of water.

Cole threw his leg over the animal and

climbed down. He enjoyed the feel of the horse beneath him, the power of the animal just as he did his Harley. The only thing sweeter was a woman beneath him. An image of Joey flashed into his mind, and he imagined her spread on the grassy slope of the hill, naked and ready to be ridden.

The brief image played havoc with his concentration. Sexual fantasies didn't belong in the middle of this case.

He stroked Apache's mane then began to unfasten his saddlebags as his half brothers approached. "Thanks, buddy, you did good today." While he'd prefer to stay and brush down the horse himself, he turned him over to the stable hand so he could deal with the Rangers.

"Did you have any luck?" Zane asked.

He wasn't lucky, he was a damn good tracker. But he refused to get into a pissing contest with the McKinneys. "I found the bullet, and collected a few other fibers that might help. Also took some footprints. They're partials but you might get something from them."

"Great." Sloan smiled, and Cole realized

he resembled Jim McKinney. He wondered if Sloan was as smooth with the women.

"With that bullet, maybe we can determine who shot Carley and make an arrest," Sloan said. "That SOB needs to pay."

"Right," Zane said. "Cole, give me everything you found, and I'll send it to the crime lab."

Cole frowned. "I could have brought it over. No need for you to have wasted time waiting around." *Unless you didn't trust me.*

"You did your job," Zane said. "We can take it from here."

Cole narrowed his eyes as he handed over the evidence bags. "Excuse me?"

"We can handle the investigation," Sloan said. "We just needed some help in tracking this down."

"You mean you're dismissing me from the case now?" Cole asked in a hard voice. "But I just got here."

His brothers exchanged an odd look that raised Cole's suspicions.

"Why do you want me gone? Is there something you guys are covering up? Something about Jim McKinney?"

"No," Zane said a little too quickly.

Cole didn't believe them. "You have new evidence against him, don't you? What is it? Did Stella tell you something? Is that why she had a breakdown? She finally admitted the truth, that he killed Lou Anne Wallace?"

A muscle ticked in Zane's jaw, and Cole realized he'd hit the nail on the head.

"No," Sloan barked. "But you'd probably like to see him fry, wouldn't you? You've hated him all these years, and you want to see him suffer."

A knot of fury balled in Cole's stomach. He hadn't expected anything but animosity from his brothers. Yet he had hoped they'd be fair.

"I'm a Ranger, same as you," he said harshly. "Jim McKinney means nothing to me, one way or the other. So you're wrong. I don't want to see him locked up. Nor do I want him to walk away if he's guilty." He grabbed his saddlebags and slung them over his shoulder. "You see, McKinneys. I'm not caught up in your family drama the way you are. And as far as *our* father goes, frankly I don't give a damn what happens to him."

Furious, he stalked toward his Harley, hung the bags across the back, grabbed his helmet and yanked it on. Then he tore down the graveled driveway, spitting dust and rocks behind his wheels.

Still, the silver star of Texas he'd found, the one he thought belonged to Jim McKinney, burned his pocket, taunting him with doubt as he headed back into town.

"NO JUSTICE in Justice—that seems to be the recurring theme the local residents are complaining about here in Tarrant County, Texas." Dennison lowered the mike to a white-haired lady in a purple knit pantsuit. "Do you agree, ma'am?"

She fluttered an age-spotted hand to her throat. "It seems that way. Poor Sarah Wallace strangled with her own purse strap."

The lady beside her clutched her handbag under her arm as if she feared the killer might do the same thing to her. "We just want to be safe again," the little woman said.

"The worst part is knowing that it's the same man who killed Lou Anne Wallace sixteen years ago." They both darted furtive looks across the street. "What if he's been here all this time, acting like he's one of us, and we never knew it!"

"I thought that Jim McKinney probably killed Lou Anne," the first woman interjected. "Or maybe his wife did out of jealousy. He sure did shame poor Stella."

"I just hope Jim's boys can be fair and do the right thing if they have to arrest their father," the second woman said. "Such a scandal."

"Do you ladies believe this case is connected to the Hendricks baby kidnapping and murder?" Dennison asked.

"Oh, my word, yes." They both sputtered.

"Leland Hendricks has more money than God now," the second woman chirped. "He'll probably pay his way out of it this time just like he did back then."

Joey clenched her jaw. She understood the women's concerns. Hadn't she thought the same thing herself?

But hearing her father slandered again hurt more than she wanted to admit.

Still, if she confronted Dennison now, it would appear as if she was defending her father. The best defense would be to find out the truth.

Spotting the bar nearby, she dashed inside. Maybe someone here might offer insight into the past.

A little early for hard liquor, she ordered a beer and claimed a seat at the bar. A few locals played pool in the back while the jukebox blared out country tunes. The waitress who'd flirted with Cole frowned at her, while a middle-aged man in a suit took a chair beside her, and a man in jeans and a cowboy shirt and hat took the other.

"Bud, I'm Joey Hendricks," she said to the bartender.

"I know who you are, honey. I saw you on the news."

She grimaced at the pet name. But she wanted answers and honey caught more flies than vinegar so she smiled. "How long have you been in Justice?"

"I grew up here," Bud said as he wiped the counter. "Owned this bar for the last twenty years."

"So you must know everyone in town?"

"Pretty much." He gestured around the

smoky room and dark corners. "People come here to let down and relax."

"And hook up," Joey said with a smile.

He shrugged. "Nothing wrong in that."

"Not if you're single."

Bud leaned forward, propping himself on his elbows. "I mind my own business. If I don't, I lose customers."

Joey nodded. "Did Jim McKinney meet Lou Anne Wallace here sixteen years ago?"

He poured a scotch for the suited man and a glass of merlot for the lady who'd joined him, then turned back to her. "They didn't exactly keep their affair a secret. Jim liked women. Period."

"So Lou Anne wasn't his only lover?"

"Just the last."

Joey stewed over that comment. She'd always wondered if Stella might have killed Lou Anne out of jealousy or revenge for screwing her husband. But if Jim had another woman on the side, that lady might not have liked the competition.

Bud's tone grew hushed. "Lou Anne's marriage to Leland didn't stop her from giving up men."

"Jim wasn't the only man she fooled around with?"

He grunted sarcastically, then turned away to handle an order from the waitress.

Joey pondered this information. Maybe Jim's lover wanted to get rid of Lou Anne. Or what if one of Lou Anne's lovers or their wives knocked her off? Had the police explored that theory?

But who else had slept with Jim McKinney? And what about Lou Anne? Who else had she taken to her bed?

Would her father know?

Her head throbbed at the thought of asking him. But she had to follow through on the possibility. She'd question him tomorrow.

Exhausted, she thanked Bud, paid for her beer, then crossed the street to the inn. Cole's Harley sat in front of the building, and she contemplated knocking on his door to see if he'd found anything new. But it was late, and if she did, she'd suffer the same dilemma as the night before.

Better to confront him in the morning when she wasn't feeling so vulnerable. And when the sight or smell of him wouldn't keep her awake all night again with longing.

She entered the inn, and veered into the stairwell to go to the second floor. Darkness bathed the hallway, and behind her, she thought she detected a footstep. The floor creaked, and she spun around, searching the darkness.

"Who's there?"

Silence stretched for a heartbeat, the whisper of someone's breathing tainting the quiet. Joey clutched her purse, wishing she had brought her gun with her instead of leaving it in the room. Bracing herself for an attack, she hurried up the steps. The footsteps sounded behind her, picking up their pace, grating on her nerves. Finally she burst through the door to the hallway, jammed the key into her room and vaulted inside. Her breath caught as she slammed the door and leaned against it. The room was pitch-dark, the air hot and sticky.

A shadow caught her eye, and she realized she wasn't alone.

She opened her mouth to scream, and reached for the doorknob, but the intruder grabbed her around the neck, cutting off her air with the heel of his hand. He clamped his other hand over her mouth and dragged her against him. "Stop nosing around, or your mother is going to get hurt."

Chapter Six

Cole swore as he threw his saddlebags on the floor of the inn room. How dare Zane and Sloan McKinney dismiss him as if he was some lackey they didn't want to be bothered with any longer. He'd come a long way to help them and that was the thanks he got.

Not that he expected a dinner invitation at the family table, but they obviously couldn't wait to see him ride out of town. Of course, then they could go about their business as always and pretend that he didn't exist the way they'd done all his life.

The way Jim McKinney had.

His throat thickened with emotions as he ran his thumb over his pocket where he'd stored the badge he'd found in the woods. Heat emanated from the metal, reminding him that he was crossing the line not turning over evidence. Was the man really worth him risking his own reputation as a Ranger? He could argue that he'd been concerned about what Sloan and Zane would do with the badge, that they might cover for their father.

But was that true? Or did some small part of him want to exonerate Jim McKinney himself?

No. He didn't give a damn about the man who'd abandoned him and his mother.

If he were guilty, he'd arrest him and see that he fried for his wrongdoings.

Bitterness knocked at the shell of apathy he'd carved around his heart, but he tamped it down. Not caring was the best defense against them all. Becoming emotional would only make him weak. Make them think he wanted to be part of the McKinneys. That he actually missed being a member of their family.

How the hell could he miss something he'd never had?

His family consisted of his mother. That was all he needed. All he ever would.

Being alone suited him fine. He had no one to answer to. No one to take care of. No one to worry about when he was on the job.

No one to warm his bed.

An image of Joey Hendricks and those mile-long legs came to mind, and he turned toward the door. Maybe he'd pay her a visit tonight before he left. See what she'd found out today.

Ask her if she'd like to share a drink before bedtime. And then...what?

Sleep with him before he hit the road?

A smile curved his mouth, and he opened the door and stepped into the hall. But just as he raised his hand to knock, he heard a noise from inside her room. A table being bumped. Something crashed. Scuffling. Then a scream.

His heart hammered into overdrive.

"Joey!" He jiggled the doorknob but it was locked. Another scream rent the air and a loud *thunk*. Someone was definitely in the room.

Joey was in trouble.

He slid his gun from his ankle holster, then slammed his shoulder against the door with all his force.

JOEY SWUNG HER ELBOW backward into the man's stomach. He grunted, then shoved her to the floor on her knees. She twisted and tried to see his face, but he kicked her in the back, and she doubled over in pain. God, if she could only reach her gun.

"Joey!" Cole's voice reverberated through the haze, and she heard his body slam against the door, jarring the wood and echoing off the walls.

Her attacker yanked her head backward by her hair and pushed a gun to the base of her skull. "Move and you die."

She froze, breathing hard, her mind racing. "Who are you? Why are you doing this?"

"If you care about your mother, steer the Rangers away from her."

Her mind raced. She couldn't believe she'd let this creep get the best of her. If she grabbed his ankle and tripped him, she might have a chance. But he might press the trigger, and she'd be dead.

Dying was not in her plans tonight.

"Do you understand?" He lifted his foot, and stomped her back again with his boot.

Pain split her lower extremities, and she cried out, sucking in air to breathe through the agony. "Yes…"

Growling something in Spanish, he kicked her shoulder so hard that tears trickled down her cheeks, and she slumped to the floor, fighting nausea.

Hugging her arms around her middle, she dragged in deep breaths, battling against the need to pass out as he leaped out the window.

Cole slammed the door again, and it swung open with a vicious *whoosh*. His boots pounded on the floor as he ran inside. She glanced sideways, crawled to her hands and knees, but the room was still spinning. "Go get him!" she snarled between clenched teeth.

"Dammit!" Cole checked the window, then ran back and knelt beside her. "Joey, are you all right?"

"Yes, I said go after him!"

"Let me call 911 and get security!"

"No, I'll call security. Go after the bastard!"

Cole glared at her, but jumped up and

vaulted toward the door to give chase. She struggled to drag herself upright while he disappeared out the door.

WEAPON DRAWN, Cole searched the shadows near the inn for signs of Joey's attacker, but didn't see him on the street or in the bushes flanking the property. With the rising panic in town, most people had obviously chosen to stay home or turn in before dark so the streets were nearly deserted. Still, a few stragglers moved along the storefronts and town square, but no one was running or acting suspicious. A teenage couple making out beneath the awning of the drugstore. Two cowboys exiting the Last Call. An old-timer walking his dog.

Frustration clawed at Cole. The guy had slithered through town to a getaway vehicle or slunk off into the neighboring woods. His guess would be the woods.

He ventured into the thicket of trees nearest the inn, watching for movement. Animals scurried through the brush, a dog howled somewhere in the distance, and mosquitoes swarmed around his face. Storm clouds crawled above, turning the sky a more ominous black and robbing any light the moon might have offered.

Sweat trickled down his jaw as he slipped through the forest, padding slowly so as not to disturb the brush and alert the man as to his presence should he be hiding nearby. He spent a half hour searching, pausing at each turn, looking in the shadows, but came up empty.

Resigned the guy had escaped, Cole walked back through the thick woods, taking a different route in case he'd missed something. But when he reached the inn, he still hadn't spotted the man. Worried about Joey, he hurried inside the inn. A young guy who looked like he was barely twenty glanced up from the front desk with a frown.

"Where in the hell is your security guard?" Cole barked.

The boy gestured toward a gray-haired man hobbling toward them. "Miss Hendricks called. I checked her floor and the main one, but didn't find anyone."

Cole rolled his eyes. The old geezer

looked as if he was half-blind himself, and was moving like a turtle.

"Call the sheriff's office. Tell dispatch to put you through to Lieutenant Zane McKinney and Sergeant Sloan McKinney there immediately!"

"Right." The man fumbled with his flashlight, then reached for his cell phone. "I'm all over it."

Cole did not feel comforted by the thought. But he ran up the stairwell toward Joey's room anyway. He had to see her and make sure she was really all right.

When he rounded the corner, the door still stood ajar. Dammit, she should have locked it. What was she thinking?

Ready to ream into her, he barreled inside. She was sitting on the bed in a crouched position as if she was in pain. But she held a .38 in her shaky hands, and it was aimed at him.

JOEY'S HANDS trembled as she fixed the gun on the silhouette in the doorway. She'd heard the footsteps and hoped it was Cole, but she refused to be caught off guard again.

"Joey?" The shadow slowly held up a hand. "It's me, Cole. Put down the gun slowly."

Her breath tumbled from her mouth, full of relief, and she finally allowed herself to relax. Still, her hand jerked as she lowered the weapon. "Did you catch him?"

Cole shook his head, his expression stony as he moved into the room. "I searched the neighboring streets and woods, but he disappeared. "Are you all right?"

No, she was a mess, but she hated to admit it. As tough as she'd always perceived herself to be, and although she had taken self-defense classes, a real attack was different from a staged one in a practice setting.

"Did you call for an ambulance?"

"I don't need a doctor, Cole. I'm fine."

"I don't believe you." Cole slid down onto the bed beside her, checked the safety on the gun, then placed it inside the nightstand drawer. Then he tilted her chin up with his thumb. "Where did he hurt you?"

Concern tinged his gruff voice, bringing unwanted tears to her eyes. She blinked them away, hoping he hadn't seen them, furious with herself.

"Ahh, Joey."

A sob escaped her as Cole pulled her into his arms. She collapsed against his chest, grateful not to be alone with the memories of the man who'd attacked her.

He crushed her into his arms, and stroked her hair gently as he rocked her back and forth. "Are you really all right? You don't need a doctor?"

"No…" She clutched his arms, savoring his strength and the scent of his raw masculinity.

He brushed a hand across her cheek and forced her to look at him. "Tell me what happened."

Her throat ached with the effort to hold back more tears. "I thought someone was behind me on the stairwell, so I rushed into the room and slammed the door shut. He grabbed me as soon as I came inside."

"He was inside the room when you entered?"

She nodded and leaned her head against his chest again, remembering the feel of the man's hand at her throat. Then his voice in her ear. "He told me to stop nosing around or Donna would end up hurt."

"He threatened your mother?"

"Yes."

He trailed his hand down her back, and she winced. "He did hurt you?"

"I'm just bruised."

"Let me see." His fingers went to the bottom of her shirt, but she pushed his hands away.

"Stop it, Cole. I'm fine."

"Then show me." His dark eyes dared her to prove her statement.

She ground her teeth together, and shook her head.

He reached for his cell phone. "Then I'm calling the paramedics."

"No." She rested her hand on his, waiting for him to rescind his threat, but he didn't back down. Instead he reached for her shirt again. She sucked in a sharp breath and closed her eyes, trembling as he slowly unbuttoned her shirt, and parted the fabric. Cool air kissed her skin as his fingers trailed over her body. In spite of the fact that he only meant to check her injuries, her nipples beaded beneath the flaming red lace of her bra. His own hiss told her that he noticed her reaction.

"He kicked me in the back," she said in a low voice. "And my shoulders."

"Turn around."

"Cole?"

"Do it, Joey."

His harsh voice reeked of anger. She huffed in frustration and pivoted while he examined her back. His fingers gently traced a path over the sore tissue, trailing from her shoulder blades down to her waist. Then he turned her in his arms, and she felt raw, vulnerable. Exposed.

One look down at his hands and she itched to have them stroking her other places. Quivering with need, she glanced at his eyes and saw a mixture of emotions. Desire flickered in the depths along with fury.

"I'm going to kill the SOB," he muttered.

"Cole…" He hushed her with a finger to her lips, then lowered his head and replaced his fingers with his mouth. She clung to his arms, and parted her lips for him.

COLE HAD NO IDEA what had possessed him, but one minute he was examining the bruises on Joey's beautiful body, his anger rising like a beast within him, and he'd wanted to kill the man, then the next minute he'd dragged her into his arms and fused his mouth with hers.

She tasted like beer and sin and temptation, a heady combination. Yet she'd been attacked, and needed comfort. Not to be mauled by another man. Behind him, the sound of footsteps registered. A man's voice followed.

"Excuse me. I thought this was an emergency."

Cole pulled away from Joey, and yanked her shirt together, angling himself to shield her as Zane McKinney's stern voice registered.

Hellfire and damnation. He'd come here to prove he was a professional and now his half brothers had caught him behaving anything but professionally. Joey's expression morphed somewhere between the pale shock of her attack, pain from the physical wounds and crimson from embarrassment. He stood, giving her time to rebutton her shirt while he blocked the door.

"I did ask the security guard to call you,"

Cole said. "Miss Hendricks was attacked in her room. I was just checking her injuries."

Zane's left eyebrow rose a fraction as a small smile played on his mouth. "Is that what you were doing?"

"Yes." Although the kiss had shaken him to the core. Coupled with the fact that she might have died tonight, his emotions flew into a tailspin. Pure animal lust mixed with white-hot fury rallied through him.

Joey stood and approached Zane. "A man broke into my room and threatened me, Lieutenant McKinney. Cole showed up and tried to catch him, but he managed to escape."

"Are you all right? Should I call a doctor?"

"No, I'm just bruised," Joey insisted.

"Did you see the assailant?" Zane asked.

Joey shook her head. "No, it was too dark, and he grabbed me from behind."

"Did he say anything?"

She gave Cole a wary look but nodded. "He told me to drop the investigation or my mother would get hurt."

Cole chewed the inside of his cheek. For

some reason he sensed Joey was holding something back. Had her attacker threatened her in another way?

Sloan appeared and frowned at him as he poked his head in the room. "I thought you were leaving town, Cole."

"I'm not going," he announced. "Not until we find out what's going on around here."

His brothers' reactions were exactly what he expected. Both glared at him as if the subject wasn't open for discussion. They had dismissed him, and he was supposed to comply.

But Cole had never been a compliant child. And he certainly wasn't as an adult. Like it or not, he didn't intend to leave Joey now. Not after that cataclysmic kiss. And not with the killer breathing down her neck with threats.

Chapter Seven

Joey sensed the tension between Cole and the McKinney brothers. Tension born from their parent's mistakes, a fact that had automatically set the men against each other just as the investigation put them all on opposite sides.

The next two hours whizzed by in a chaotic nightmare. Lieutenant Zane McKinney took charge, ordered a crime scene unit to search the room for trace evidence, check the security tapes and insisted that a doctor evaluate her and photograph and record her injuries. Obviously feeling displaced, Cole volunteered to drive her to the hospital and waited while she was X-rayed and processed to the letter of the law.

True, she wanted to catch her assailant, but she also knew he was probably a hired hand, not the top dog behind the crimes. And she vacillated between various interpretations of his threat. Had he meant that he would hurt Donna if she didn't steer the investigation away from her, or that exposing the truth would hurt Donna?

Both terrified her in different ways. The first that Donna might be physically harmed. The latter that Donna had actually been involved in the murders.

Anxiety hit her full force—did she believe her mother was innocent or guilty?

She wanted to think that she had been a victim…but Donna had been drinking years ago when Lou Anne had been killed, and had hated Lou Anne. She'd had motive, opportunity and the capabilities to pull it off. She was physically fit, could shoot a gun and she'd been desperate to regain custody of her son. Getting rid of Lou Anne and framing Leland for the crime would have been her ticket to reverse the court decision.

A dull ache settled in her chest at the thought. She didn't want to believe that her mother had committed murder or tried to cover up by shooting the sheriff and burning down the jail.

Tears pricked at her eyelids, and she blinked them away as she walked to the waiting room to meet Cole. She'd never admitted her feelings to anyone, not even herself. But for years, she had craved Donna's affection and love.

Joey's childhood haunted her. She'd wondered why Donna had preferred booze to tucking her children in at night. Why at thirteen, when she'd been struggling with adolescence, with being a tomboy and a gangly too-tall teenager, Donna had fallen into depression and alcohol.

And Joey and Justin had been caught in a tug-of-war that followed. Pawns in the vindictive battle Donna and Leland had waged against one another.

But Justin had lost the most.

Cole stood by the waiting room door with a cup of coffee in hand, his expression solemn. "Everything all right?"

How could it be when one or both of her parents might be killers?

She nodded, though, determined to see this investigation through. "I'm free to go now."

"Good. I told the doc to send the trace to our lab. Maybe we'll get evidence to nail this guy."

Joey remained silent as they walked out to the car. The summer heat was oppressive, making her clothes stick to her skin. The smell of her attacker still clung to her, or maybe it was the scent of her own fear. She desperately wanted a shower and some rest. But when she closed her eyes, she knew she would see that shadow lunge for her. She'd feel his hands tightening around her throat, and the gun pressed at the base of her skull.

A shudder tore through her as she climbed in the car Cole had borrowed from the Rangers. "Did you think of anything else about your attacker?" Cole asked.

Joey massaged her temple and closed her eyes, reliving the assault. "He had an Hispanic accent." She jerked her eyes open. "I didn't think about that at the time."

"Probably a hired hand. Maybe an illegal."

Which meant he'd be impossible to find. But she'd been right—he was working for someone else. But whom?

"Unfortunately he ducked the security cameras." Cole's lips curled into a snarl. "What about earlier tonight? Did you talk to anyone who might have followed you?"

She tried to remember if she'd seen anyone watching her at the bar. "I had a beer at the Last Call and talked to Bud for a while."

Cole veered onto the street to the inn. "Learn anything new?"

"He suggested that both Jim McKinney and Lou Anne Wallace had other affairs."

Cole grunted. "I'm not surprised."

"Then it's possible that one of their lovers might have killed Lou Anne."

"It sounds feasible. Of course Stella had reason to want Lou Anne dead, too."

"I think we should talk to both of them," Joey said.

Cole chuckled sarcastically. "I'm sure she'll welcome seeing me."

"I can question her if you want, Cole."

He shrugged. "I don't need coddling,

Joey. Hell, maybe I'll pay Jim McKinney a visit. It's time I met the man."

Joey squeezed his hand. In spite of the unbearable heat, the chill that had pervaded her earlier grew in intensity. They both had to face their fathers with difficult questions.

Lou Anne's affair with Jim had been hard on Leland's ego. And if she'd threatened to report his plan to the police or Donna, he had motive to kill Lou Anne. Another affair would rub salt into his wounds and might have sent him over the edge.

But would her own father hire someone to attack her to protect himself or Donna?

She had to know the truth. She only hoped she could live with whatever she discovered.

WHEN COLE ESCORTED Joey back into the inn, the crime scene unit was finishing processing the room.

"Get your things and we'll move you," Cole said.

Joey nodded and hurried to repack her suitcase while Cole arranged for a room, then conferred with Zane and Sloan in the hall. "Did you find anything?"

Zane shrugged. "Sorry. No prints. He must have worn gloves."

"We received word about the bullet you found in the woods," Sloan said. "Forensics lifted a partial and is running it now. If we're lucky, the print is in the system. If not, at least when we catch this guy, we'll have something to use as a comparison."

"Let me know if you get a hit or a name," Cole said. He thought about the silver star he'd found in the woods. If Jim was guilty of two murders, had he hired someone to kill Joey? Or maybe to scare her away?

Zane cleared his throat. "Look, Cole, we appreciate your help, but we can handle the situation now."

"I'm not leaving town," Cole said. "Not while Joey is in danger."

"I didn't know you two were that close," Zane said.

Cole narrowed his eyes. "We're not. But it looks like she might need protection. That comes with our job title, doesn't it, Lieutenant?"

Zane grunted, but Cole thought he detected a small smile on Sloan's mouth.

They might not respect him because he was their illegitimate half brother, but he had proven his worth today. In fact, if he hadn't been around, Joey might have ended up dead.

Not a thought that settled well with him at all. The world needed more long-legged, spunky blondes.

Joey appeared at the door, ducked beneath the crime scene tape and halted.

"How are you now, Miss Hendricks?" Zane asked.

"I'm fine, just exhausted."

"Do you want me to post one of the deputies outside your door?" Zane asked.

Joey's eyes widened. "I don't think that will be necessary. I'll lock the room and be fine."

"By the way, that gun we found in the nightstand—I'm assuming you have a license to carry, and that you know how to use it?" Sloan asked.

"Yes, I do." Joey's mouth tightened. "And if I could have gotten to it, that guy wouldn't have escaped."

"Where'd you learn to shoot?" Zane asked.

Joey stiffened.

"Never mind," Zane said with a small smile. "I'm sure Donna taught you."

"As a matter of fact, she did," Joey said. "And I'm a damn good shot, too."

"I'm sure you are," Zane said. "But in light of tonight's events, perhaps you should leave town."

"Good try, Lieutenant McKinney, but I'm here at the governor's request," Joey said. "And I don't intend to leave until this investigation is complete."

Zane ran a hand through his hair. "Well, then, it seems we all want the same thing."

Cole grunted. He doubted it. Zane and Sloan wanted to see their father exonerated, and Joey's father or mother or both convicted for the crime. They were working with the grand jury now to try to get an indictment against Leland.

"Call me if there are any more problems," Zane said.

Cole hooked his thumbs in his belt loops. "Let me know what you find out from forensics."

Zane nodded, then he and Sloan left. Cole

turned to Joey, his gaze zeroing in on the red bruise marks around her neck. Anger ripped through him.

Cole unlocked the door to the room on the opposite side of his, then checked the interior, making certain the locks on the windows were secure. Joey stowed her suitcase on the floor and a small toiletry bag inside the bathroom.

The antique furniture and braided rug made the room look more like a guest room in someone's home than a hotel. And that bed looked damn inviting…

It was big enough for two, easily.

Joey tugged a strand of her blond hair behind her ear and sank onto the quilt, obviously exhausted.

"You could stay in my room with me," Cole offered.

Joey nearly choked on a laugh. "You are smooth, Cole McKinney."

Not smooth enough or he would already have bedded her.

Which would have made him the bastard everyone assumed him to be. Maybe he was more like Jim McKinney than he wanted to believe.

Still, she appeared so vulnerable and… sweet that he walked toward her, leaned over and threaded his fingers into the soft tresses of her hair. It felt like silk and satin and every man's wildest dreams. He imagined it draped across his bare belly, his hands sliding down to cup her breasts and suck on her lips, and his sex hardened.

She parted her mouth and licked the rosy petaled outline of her lips, taunting him with a memory of that earlier kiss.

"Cole?"

Her sultry whisper echoed with need. Desire. Hunger.

"I should go now," he said, struggling to resist her.

"Yes, you probably should."

He nodded but his feet refused to move.

Her chest rose and fell with her breathing, drawing his eye to the soft swell of her cleavage. Underneath that shirt there were bruises.

But also a beautiful body. And melon-sized globes encased in red lace.

Puckered nipples he wanted to taste and suckle.

Hell.

He leaned over and captured her mouth with his. She made a small throaty sound like a whimper, then opened to him as if in invitation. He teased her lips apart with his tongue, then delved inside and explored her mouth again. She tasted hot and passionate, and erotic sensations exploded in the tiny tongue thrusts that met his lips.

Instantly unsettled by the strength of his reaction, he pulled back and stared at her eyes. They were slitted, sleepy looking, sensual. Aroused.

"Why did you do that?" she whispered.

He murmured the only thing he could. The truth. "Because I had to."

Shaken even more by that thought, he stalked out the door, his declaration reverberating in his ears.

Cole had always loved women. Had been a player.

But he had never actually loved any woman over another, or let a female get to him. He'd never felt this protective or... needy.

And he couldn't now.

Especially not with Joey Hendricks. Hell, she was the daughter of not just one, but two prime suspects in the mystery he'd come here to unravel. She was the last damn woman he needed to get involved with.

His detective instincts surged to life, raising suspicions. Dammit. Joey was a smart woman. Maybe she was here to distract him and his half brothers from looking at her parents as suspects. She'd obviously prefer Jim McKinney be arrested instead.

He had to watch her. Gain access to any information she uncovered. And staying close to her was the only way to do that.

JIM MCKINNEY stared at his wife's frail body as she slept. The hospital bed swallowed her ninety pounds of bones, and her pallor was as white as the pristine sheets she lay upon. The scent of antiseptic and medicine and the clinking of hospital machinery and nurses' voices echoed in the sterile halls, reminding him that Stella was sick.

And that he was to blame for her illness.

He dropped his head into his splayed

hands, guilt weighing on him. He hated what their marriage and life had become. When they'd first wed, Stella had been a beautiful girl. He'd thought he loved her. Yet he'd quickly realized that he was flawed, that she wasn't enough. He didn't intend to make excuses for his behavior, but she had been spoiled, stubborn and had insisted on having everything her way. In and out of the bedroom.

The second part he could take, but the first—her bossiness as well as her lack of interest in sex had been enough to send him looking for satisfaction elsewhere. At least that was how he'd justified his indiscretions.

But then he'd hooked up with Lou Anne, she had been murdered, and his life had gone downhill fast.

Stella mumbled something, her eyelids fluttering as she wrestled with the covers. He adjusted the blanket, trying to soothe her from whatever demons dogged her.

Her eyes opened momentarily, but her gaze looked clouded as if she had no idea where she was or what was happening to her.

"Rest now, Stella."

She muttered something incoherent, then mumbled the word "bastard." She meant both him and Cole. She'd never forgiven him for having another child, and when she heard that Cole was coming to town, she was certain he intended to rub his father's indiscretions in her face. To Stella, appearance meant everything.

For that reason, he'd wondered why she'd stayed with him all these years. He'd lost his job, his respect and friends over the murder charges and he'd never regained them.

Of course, staying with him was her way of punishing him. Each day her anger and bitterness ate at her. She'd used it to hold onto him.

He scrubbed a hand over his face, walked to the window and looked out at the mottled storm clouds. Sweat rolled down his neck and collar as he wondered what his boys had found when they'd searched the woods.

All three of his boys—Rangers.

He couldn't believe he'd shamed them by losing his position, yet they'd all joined the Rangers anyway. God, he'd failed at his job. Failed his wife. His boys. Especially Cole…

He'd heard that Sarah had evidence that might help them find Lou Anne's killer.

Why had she called him that night? To tell him that she knew he had killed her mother? Or had she discovered something to prove his innocence?

If only he could remember what happened the night Lou Anne died…

All he recalled was his argument with Stella, her vicious put-downs. And his plans to assuage his ego with Lou Anne's luscious body. And then the booze…

If he had killed Lou Anne, it was time he learned the truth. Half the town, including his wife, had tried and convicted him in their minds anyway. And he'd resigned from the Rangers before they'd forced him out. Now he spent his days stacking groceries in a little store. And staring at a shell of a woman who no longer loved him. How much worse could prison be?

Still, guilt drew him to Stella. She had lied about her whereabouts that night—she hadn't had an alibi. Sometimes he wondered if he'd repressed the memory because he'd witnessed her kill Lou Anne.

When he'd mentioned using a psychiatrist to jog his memory, Stella had become violently upset, then broken down. Was she afraid of what he would remember because it might implicate her as the killer?

Chapter Eight

Sleep eluded Joey for hours after Cole said good night. Long into the hot, sultry evening, she lay awake, tossing, turning in the big double bed. The image of her attacker approaching tormented her. The feel of his hands on her throat, his breath against her ear…

The fear that he might return and kill her this time.

Shivering, she rolled to her side and stared at the blank wall. The ceiling fan whirled above, stirring the tepid air. Outside, the soft sound of cicadas and crickets chirped in the night. She listened for any indication that Cole might still be awake and swore she could almost hear his breathing through the paper-thin walls.

She imagined his hands touching her instead of the other man's vile grip, and erotic sensations splintered through her. Only that thin piece of plywood and insulation separated her from the sexiest man she'd ever met. That and her own resolve to stay professional and not sleep with him. Cole was too masculine, too hot, too damn sexy for his own good. He'd be a dynamite lover in bed. Would soothe her fears for the night. Ignite her senses. Make her forget all about that man who'd tried to choke her and that her parents might be guilty of murder.

But then he'd go his way and she'd be all alone again.

Not that Joey Hendricks needed anyone. She'd been alone for years. Ever since she was a kid really. Donna had been too absorbed in her drinking to notice anything she did. And Leland...he'd been as addicted to women as Donna had been to booze.

She closed her eyes, and pressed her fingers to her lips. Her mouth still tingled from the feel of Cole McKinney's lips on her skin.

She was starting to understand addiction—she couldn't stop thinking about the big handsome man. His kisses teased her to forget her ethics. To accept one night if that was all he could offer.

She shoved away the covers. Heavens, the room was hot. Was Cole sweating next door, too? Was he already asleep, alone in the bed?

Naked with the sheets kicked off?

She hissed, irritated and aroused at the sensual picture that image painted in her mind's eye. He was so tall that she imagined his arms sprawled above his head. His bronzed skin slick with perspiration. His long legs dangling over the side of the bed. His sex thick and swollen, jutting out as if needing to be stroked.

What would he do if she knocked on his door? Would he tell her to go away? Or would he pull her into his arms? Take her to bed and kiss away her anxiety? Stroke her with those wide, masculine hands? Crawl on top of her and love her until she didn't remember her own name?

Mercy. One night with him would be more exciting than all the nights she'd spent with other men combined. She'd been pretty socially inept at flirting when she was young and the men she'd finally connected with later on in life hadn't exactly been stellar lovers. Of course, maybe she hadn't excited them all that much.

Or maybe they were the wrong men.

But Cole…she had no doubt in her mind that he would please her in bed. She closed her eyes, imagined him sliding beneath the covers. She could almost feel his body brushing hers, his heat radiating her skin, him pulsing inside her…

COLE LISTENED for sounds of trouble next door, and knew that *he* was in the one in trouble. All he could think about was Joey Hendricks. How much he wanted her body. How it would feel beneath him. How her breasts would fit inside his hands.

How he would fit inside her.

His sex hardened and thickened, and sweat broke out on his skin. He should take a cold shower. Or maybe go for a run. A long, exhausting one that would tire his muscles, his wandering mind and his aching libido.

But then Joey would be alone.

And although the feisty, independent smart woman would balk at the idea of a bodyguard, he'd assigned himself the job. And her body was a damn fine one to have to watch.

Hmm, might not be a bad job at all.

He'd been undercover near the border and in some god-awful places the last year. Being inside *her* would prove to be a tempting reprieve and would feel like heaven to a man who'd come from hell.

Dammit. He had to stop thinking like that. Like Jim McKinney would think.

Was he no better than the bastard man who'd sired him?

His brothers didn't want him or Joey on the case. Granted, her story about handling the media had credit, but it was also an excuse. She was going to dig into the investigation here, and he would be right by her side. Helping her question the locals. Finding answers. Protecting her. Making sure she didn't cover up the truth.

And taking her to bed.

His feet hit the floor and he forced himself to do some push-ups.

He would *not* take her to bed.

But he would guard her delectable body with his life.

He pumped himself through two hundred push-ups, then flicked on a light and sat down to study the files. Jim McKinney had been a major suspect in the original murder.

And Cole had assumed he was guilty. After all, a man who cheated on his wife, impregnated another woman and never acknowledged his third son didn't exactly merit trust or respect.

Had his mother believed in Jim's innocence? Or had she stayed away and not encouraged a relationship between him and Cole because she'd thought that Jim might possess a violent streak? That he was dangerous?

But what was Jim's motive? Had Lou Anne wanted Jim to leave Stella and marry her? That didn't make sense. Then again, Lou Anne might have married Leland Hendricks for his money, then discovered the man was tapped out to the nines, and decided Jim was a better catch. But according to the files, Lou Anne had her own money, money she'd kept secret from Leland. Or had he discovered the funds and killed her hoping to gain access to her accounts?

He'd follow up when he interrogated Leland. And he'd ask his father about his affairs when he finally met him. If Lou Anne had wanted more than he was willing to give.

Willing—or capable?

His own panicked reaction to commitment made guilt tug at his chest. A small part of him understood Jim's wandering eye, his love for women. The very reason Cole had never married. If he ever did, it would be for life. He would not cheat on a woman or knock up some girl and leave her in the wind, or a child without a father. Not to bear the shame and feelings of unworthiness that got tangled in a child's mind when he was unwanted.

And what about other lovers that Jim, Leland or Lou Anne might have had? Joey had mentioned the possibility. Who else had Lou Anne slept with? Had Jim been keeping another woman on the side? Had Leland decided that taking another woman to his bed might be ample payback for his wife's indiscretions?

He heard the bed squeak next door and realized Joey might still be awake. His body twitched with arousal at the mere thought of her lying in the bed. In spite of the air conditioner, he was so damn hot. Would she be wearing a skimpy, transparent gown? Something silky and flimsy?

Or maybe nothing at all?

He moaned in frustration, then dropped to the floor again, and lapsed into another fit of push-ups. No way would he get any sleep tonight.

JOEY HUGGED her arms around her and finally dozed into a fitful sleep. But in her sleep, once again the past rose to haunt her.

JOEY HATED being a teenager.

In fact she hated everything about her life. She was thirteen and flat-chested. Her feet were too big for her gangly body. And she was a big klutz, especially in front of the boys.

Todd Johnson had belly laughed at her

tonight. And she'd been trying so hard to impress him.

Tears dribbled down her face as she ran up the driveway to her father's new house. She hated the cold monstrosity. Hated the fact that her mother wouldn't be there, and that she and Justin had been forced to move in with her father. The lying, cheating bastard.

All she wanted to do was crawl into bed and hide for the rest of her miserable existence. She couldn't go back to school.

Or to the ranch where Todd worked.

Which meant she had to give up Chance, the palomino she loved with all her heart.

But Todd had seen her feeble attempt in the teenage rodeo competition, and she'd never live it down. She hadn't made it past the first rounds. No, she'd fallen flat on her face in the dusty ground while the mare she'd been paired with had kicked and bucked. She'd rejected her immediately just as the boys did.

Why couldn't she have been more like her mother? Donna had been a rodeo star when she was young. Agile, confident, elegant, a champion rider. Joey had seen all the trophies and admired her mother's athleticism and skill.

And Donna had most likely been a charmer, too. She was still beautiful.

Except when she was slurring her words and slit-eyed drunk.

She swiped at the tears on her face, hoping that her father wasn't in the study as she let herself in the dark, tomblike house. She didn't want to face him tonight.

The lights were off downstairs. He was probably already in bed with Lou Anne. She shuddered at the thought of what the two of them might be doing. He was so enamored with his new wife that he probably didn't even realize Joey had missed her curfew. Sometimes she wondered why he'd fought for custody when he didn't seem to know she existed. He didn't pay attention to her brother, Justin, either.

He just wanted to hurt Donna. He didn't care about his daughter, not really. Just his new whore.

She removed her boots and placed them by the door to the mudroom, then stepped in her socked feet across the marble floor to sneak upstairs. The house seemed eerily silent. No home-cooked meal scenting the kitchen. No bustling Rosa. No laughter.

Not that her parents had laughed the last few years.

Sadness welled in her chest. At first she'd been heartbroken tonight that neither he nor Donna had shown up to cheer her performance, but now she was glad they hadn't seen her disastrous fall. Of course, she hadn't really expected them to come to the event.

Ever since the bitter divorce, it was as if she was invisible. Once the marriage ended, they'd written her out of their lives. She was just a problem to deal with, a piece of rope to pull back and forth between them.

From her baby brother's room, she heard a soft cry. She paused on the back staircase, waiting to see if her father roused. But his room was on the opposite end from the nursery. The housekeeper would probably go to him.

Guilt pressed against her chest. Justin hated the new housekeeper.

The wail grew louder, and she rushed to the nursery and eased the door open. Justin stood in the crib, jerking with sobs. With the moon glinting through the window shade, she saw his chubby fists curled around the edge of the crib. Saw the tears streaming down his little face. Her heart squeezed.

"Mommy...." he whimpered. "Want Mommy."

Joey's stomach knotted. Poor little Justin. He missed their mother. At least she'd had a few good years with Donna when she was young, before the drinking and fighting with Leland had begun. Not that she blamed her mother. If her husband cheated on her like her father cheated on Donna, she'd probably be depressed, too.

No, she'd kill his sorry ass instead.

"Mommy!" Justin cried. "Want Mommy!"

"Shh, Justin, Joey's here." She forced her voice to a whisper, then carried him to the rocking chair in the corner. Justin wrestled for a minute, fussing, but she stroked his round head, smiling at the fine baby hair on his scalp, and began to sing his favorite lullaby.

Justin clutched his blue blanket in his fists. "Want Mommy…"

"I know," Joey whispered with tears in her eyes. She wanted her, too. But the judge said they had to live with Leland and his whore. So she and Justin had to stick together. She cradled him closer. She'd take care of him, always…

JOEY JERKED AWAKE, heaving with tears and rocking herself back and forth. She'd never stop missing her brother, wondering if he was dead. And if her parents had arranged Justin's kidnapping and were responsible for his death, she would help send them to jail.

What if they were overlooking a suspect? Maybe another one of her father's lovers. Or Lou Anne's.

Would he share their names with her if she asked?

Her phone jangled and she checked the number. The governor. Tempted to ignore the call, she pushed the hair from her face, but she couldn't avoid her boss. Not the governor of Texas.

She picked up the handset, not surprised to hear him rant her name.

"What in the world is going on, Joey? I saw the news. You were attacked last night?"

Hell. Dennison again. How had he found out? Was he tapped into the police scanner? "I'm fine, Governor Grange. I guess my being here is making someone nervous."

"Maybe you should come back then," he said in a concerned voice. "I'll send someone else to handle the press."

A man. No, she'd worked too darn long and hard to get this post to run with her tail tucked between her legs. "No, I can handle things. Besides, I've connected with Sergeant Cole McKinney."

"Connected?"

She swallowed, not wanting to elaborate. "Yes, he and his half brothers are estranged, so I think he may be a good source for us."

"Ahh, the bastard son with vengeance on his mind. Wonderful. He's ready to put Jim McKinney away then?"

Joey stiffened at his referral to Cole being a bastard. "Yes. And I think that Lou Anne might have been having an affair with someone else. I'm going to look into that angle today."

A long pause. Then the governor cleared his throat. "Are you sure that's smart? The evidence has pointed to Jim McKinney all along."

"And to my father," Joey said. "The other McKinney brothers are trying to get the grand jury to indict him."

"So you believe your father is innocent?"

The governor had asked her the same question before she'd left and she hadn't known how to answer. She still didn't. "I don't know. But I want the truth once and for all."

"All right." He made a noise in his throat, then Joey heard his wife's soft voice in the background. "Let me know what you find out. But be careful, Joey."

Joey agreed, then hung up and headed to the shower. She had work to do, and she desperately wanted to prove herself to the governor.

Even if it meant exposing all the dirty little secrets in Justice. Including her own family's.

BY DAWN Cole had showered and dressed. He paced the small room, anxious to confront Stella and his father.

But he didn't want to leave Joey alone.

He heard the shower water kick on in her room and groaned. The next half hour was brutally torturous as images of a naked and soaking wet Joey traipsed through his mind. Joey's perky breasts slick with soap, her nipples distended from the water's sensation, bubbles sliding down her belly, legs and thighs.

Finally he'd had enough. With his badge pinned in place to remind him of his purpose in Justice, he strode next door and knocked. Had he given her time to dress or would he find her wearing a towel, naked beneath?

Much to his disappointment, when she opened the door, she was dressed. But the short denim skirt looked feminine as hell, with a tank top that outlined her voluptuous shape. God, even clothed, she was a tempting siren, and it was only 6:00 a.m.

"What are your plans today?" he asked.

She tilted her head sideways and studied him, a sparkle of interest in her eyes that did nothing but send fire to his belly. "I'm going to eat breakfast at Donna's. Then I thought I'd visit my old man."

He nodded. "Why don't we stop by the hospital and see Stella on the way? We'll go from there to question Jim."

"You want us to go together?" Surprise tinged Joey's voice.

"After what happened last night, I'm not letting you out of my sight."

Wariness and something else flashed in her eyes—a frisson of sexual arousal? "You're going to be my bodyguard, Cole?"

"Yep. I plan to guard your body with my life," he said, allowing a teasing note to enter his voice.

Her eyes lit up. "Why doesn't that make me feel safe?"

He chuckled and leaned forward, then took her arm. "Because you know I want you," he said bluntly.

Laughter erupted from her, but she didn't back away. Instead she walked down the hall, her hips swaying as if to confirm that she liked his flirting.

He liked her, too. Which complicated the situation even more. He'd wanted women before, but he'd never actually *liked* one.

Thankfully breakfast at Donna's sobered them both from their banter. Tension thrummed through the room as soon as they entered. The locals seemed nervous, darting furtive glances around as if expecting a killer to emerge from their booth and suddenly strike.

The reporter, Harold Dennison, approached. "I heard you were assaulted last night. Care to comment, Miss Hendricks?"

Joey shrugged. "No."

He tapped his pad impatiently. "Come on, Joey. You work for the governor. An attack on you is newsworthy and you know it. Especially since your family is involved in the investigation of both the Wallace murders."

"You've already got your story," Joey said emphatically. "So buzz off, Dennison."

Anger flared in the man's beady eyes, and for a moment, Cole thought he was going to pounce on Joey. He stood abruptly, jarring the condiments on the table as his leg knocked the table edge.

"You heard the lady. Now get lost or you deal with me."

"Are you threatening me?" Dennison's eye twitched.

Cole jerked him by the collar, smiling as the man's chicken neck bobbed red. "I'm an officer of the law, mister. I can arrest you for interfering with an investigation, and make sure you get buried in some cell where you'll wish I had hurt you."

"This is not over. I will get the *whole* story." Dennison slanted a furious look at Cole but stalked off.

Cole saw Donna watching him from the corner. An odd expression flared on Rosa's face. Almost a smile as if she was pleased that he'd defended Joey.

He threw some money on the table. "Come on, Joey. We have work to do."

She took a last sip of her coffee and headed to the door. Outside, the morning air already felt stifling. Joey lifted her hair off her neck and fanned it, making him itch to kiss that soft area behind her earlobe.

But he ignored his instincts, climbed in the Rangers-issued vehicle and drove straight to the hospital. He wanted to talk to Jim, but first he'd hear Stella's side of the story. His gut tightened. Or maybe he was just stalling seeing his old man.

Joey clenched the dashboard as he parked. "Do you want me to question her?"

He shook his head. "I'm not running like my mother did," he said. "Let everyone here deal with it."

She nodded, and climbed out and they walked up to the entrance. Inside he checked with the nurses' station and asked for Stella's room number.

"I'm sorry, but only family members are allowed visitation," the nurse said.

"It's imperative that I speak with her." Cole flashed his badge. "Sergeant Cole McKinney."

The woman glanced nervously at an older nurse who shook her head. "The doctor's orders were very specific."

A man's voice echoed from the hall, and Cole froze. Zane's. Sloan's voice followed.

Ignoring the nurse's scowl, he strode down the hall. Joey followed on his heel, silent but supportive.

He spotted his half brothers standing

outside a closed door and met them with a stony look.

"What in the hell are you doing here?" Zane asked.

"I came on official business to talk to Stella."

Sloan stepped forward, arms crossed. "Our mother is not up for visitors. She's fragile and needs rest."

"As a Ranger, I have every right to question her," Cole said.

"I'm in charge of this investigation," Zane stated in a commanding voice. "And I say that you don't."

Joey cleared her throat. "As a representative of the governor's staff, I say Cole is entitled to question Stella."

Both men glared at Joey.

"Tell the governor that our mother is ill, and that she cannot be interrogated." Zane's deep voice boomed with authority as he addressed Joey. Then he hooked a thumb toward Cole. "Especially by *him*."

"That's right," Sloan interjected. "You will only upset her, Cole. She can't handle seeing you right now."

Cole gritted his teeth so hard his jaw ached. "But Stella might know something to help solve this case. And you two are covering for her."

"She's heavily medicated and incoherent," Sloan muttered.

Suddenly the door swung open, and Stella's frail form appeared. Her face looked gaunt, thin, and dark circles shadowed her large eyes. She clung to the doorway as if she might slide right down to the floor if she let go.

"Good grief, boys, what's all this shouting about?" She spotted Cole and swayed. "Why are you here? To rub my nose in my husband's indiscretions?"

The pain and tears in her voice sparked guilt to flare in Cole's chest. This woman hated his mother and him, but his mom had been a victim of Jim's wandering libido.

"No, Mrs. McKinney. I want to know if your husband killed Sarah Wallace and her mother," Cole said matter-of-factly.

Zane reached for his mother to hold her upright. "Leave us alone!" Stella whispered harshly. "Go back to your heathen mother."

Grief seared Cole. "My mother is dead. She has been for years."

"So now you want to intrude on our family?" Stella shrieked. "I won't let that happen. We already have enough trouble!" She clutched both her sons as if they were anchors. "Make him leave now, please, make him go away."

Cole felt Joey's hand on his arm, but he eased away from her touch. "I'm sorry, Mrs. McKinney—"

Suddenly Harold Dennison appeared as if he'd emerged from the woodwork, and a camera flash blinded Cole. Dennison snapped more pictures in rapid succession, capturing Stella's frantic screams. Sloan tried to coax his mother into the room while Zane snarled at Dennison. "Get the hell out of here!"

"You can't stop me from reporting the news," Dennison said with a smirk on his face.

"You have no right to follow Texas Rangers or spy on my family," Zane barked.

Joey reached for Dennison's arm. "Harold, you can't print those photos—"

Dennison shook his finger at them. "You may be Rangers, but your family is dead center in the middle of these murders, and if you're covering for them, you'll be exposed."

Zane shoved Dennison toward the door. "We do not have to answer to you. We're the law here."

"Yes, you do answer to me," Dennison wailed. "The public has a right to the truth. The citizens of Justice are terrified."

"Get out!" Zane yelled.

Stella sobbed against Sloan, while he tried to soothe her pitiful cries.

Behind them footfalls pounded the floor. Boots. Then a commanding voice. "What in the Lord's name is going on?"

Zane hauled Dennison toward the exit.

Cole's stomach clenched. Jim McKinney stalked toward him wearing a pearl-gray Stetson, jeans, a white shirt and tie—dressed like a Ranger. Except his badge was missing.

A tail of a rattler dangled from the silver rope hatband. His hair was slightly graying and his back slightly bowed, but he still seemed formidable, a stranger who obviously didn't want Dennison or him around.

A cold, shocked look settled on Jim's face as his blue eyes met Cole's.

Cole forced steel to his backbone and tried to ignore Stella's shrieking. After all these years, it was time to introduce himself to the man who'd sired him and treated him as if he was a piece of garbage.

Chapter Nine

Joey tried to remain calm as the tension escalated between the McKinneys. Stella looked as if she might faint any minute, and when Zane returned, a vein bulged in his neck. He would tear Cole apart if he upset her further.

Compassion for Cole stirred her own anger at the circumstances. He had been an innocent baby born from an affair and had been cast away from his rightful father. It wasn't fair. He deserved the same love and benefits Zane and Sloan had received, but instead had suffered their disdain, as well as ridicule from others.

"You need to leave, Cole," Zane said. "You've caused enough damage as it is."

"He's right." Sloan tried to coax an hysterical Stella back inside the room.

A flash of pain mixed with anger on Cole's face. Joey felt the injustice of his brothers' words and wanted to defend him, but also understood Zane and Sloan's predicament. They were simply protecting their ill mother.

Still, Cole wasn't the villain.

His expression changed from anger to sympathy as Stella leaned against Sloan and nearly passed out, raising Joey's admiration for him more.

"Put your mother back to bed." Jim gestured toward Sloan and Zane, then turned a harsh look on Cole. "You shouldn't have come here, Cole."

"I realize none of you want me around. But I'm a Texas Ranger, too." He tapped his badge. "I'm sworn to uphold the law with this badge, and I intend to get to the truth."

Jim's mouth flattened into a thin line. "Then let's go somewhere and talk."

Zane reached for his father's arm as Sloan ushered his mother inside the room and shut the door. "Dad, you don't have to do this."

Jim tipped his Stetson back and absentmindedly rubbed a hand over his shirt where his badge would have been. Joey had seen Cole make the same gesture more than once. Sloan and Zane did the same thing.

Maybe the men were more alike than they realized.

"Fine," Cole said. "Lead the way."

"There's a coffee shop around the corner." Jim glanced at Joey, his graying eyebrows arched. "I heard the governor sent you."

"Yes, and she's coming with us," Cole said in a voice that invited no argument.

"Cole, if you want time alone, I'll meet you later," Joey offered.

Cole shook his head. "No, there's nothing we have to say that you shouldn't hear. After all, you're overseeing the investigation."

Jim shifted on the balls of his feet, looking nervous, but nodded abruptly and led the way down the stairs to a coffee shop adjoining the hospital. When they all had steaming cups of coffee in hand, they claimed a booth.

"All right, Cole, what do you want to ask?" Jim said.

Emotions tinged his eyes, telling Joey more about Jim McKinney than he wanted to reveal. He was sizing up Cole, soaking in details about him as a parent would a long-lost child. He was glad to finally meet his third son. That he had regrets, not just about the investigation, but about his illegitimate child. He wanted to know more about him, to reach out and touch him.

He wanted to say things that he'd never say, especially in front of her. Maybe never.

Because he didn't think he had a right.

And he didn't. Not after he'd abandoned Cole all his life.

And Cole—she sensed he wanted more, too, but he wouldn't allow himself to ask for it.

The reasons came to her with undying clarity. Cole had built walls of steel around his heart to protect himself just as she had. He was afraid of being rejected. Of being hurt. Of not being wanted.

She sipped her coffee, and blinked back tears. Or maybe she was projecting her feelings and needs onto Cole because she was thinking about her impending reunion with her own estranged father.

Either way, Cole McKinney touched something deep inside her, something she hadn't expected to feel.

COLE HATED HIMSELF for caring what Jim McKinney thought of him, but he'd imagined this meeting for so long that he needed time to absorb the moment as they settled into their seats. He wanted his father to see that he'd achieved professional status and was on the same level as Sloan and Zane, Jim's *real* sons.

But of course, his mere presence had rocked the tight little family unit. And the fact that he'd upset the fragile Stella McKinney had not won him favors.

Dammit, he even felt sorry for Stella himself. She was pitiful.

But she also might be a murderer. Or hiding one—her own husband.

Hell, had any one of them considered how his own mother had dealt with raising a child alone? Granted, having an affair with a married man wasn't exactly something to admire, but it took two to tango, and she'd been left holding the responsibility on her lonesome.

Had Jim ever wondered what had happened to him after his mother's death? When he'd been all alone…

Jim could have at least sent flowers to his mother's grave.

Jim cleared his throat. "All right, Cole. Why did you really come?"

"To help track down Sarah Wallace's killer."

Jim's blue eyes narrowed.

"You didn't know that your two sons requested my help?"

Jim shook his head. "Things have been crazy around here with the fire and the sheriff being shot."

"Exactly." He glanced at Joey and saw her watching him. Maybe he should have left her at the inn so she wouldn't have witnessed his humiliation, but he'd run from Justice and his family long enough. He refused to be ignored anymore.

"I suppose you've read all the reports on the investigation," Jim said in a low voice.

Cole nodded. "Did you kill Sarah Wallace?"

Jim gave him a sharp look. "You don't pull any punches, do you?"

"No. Someone also attacked Miss Hendricks last night. They either wanted to kill her or scare her off. Did you hire someone to do that?"

"No."

"Did you kill Sarah Wallace?" he asked again.

Jim shook his head. "No."

"What about Lou Anne?"

Silence registered, full of tension. Jim removed his Stetson and ran a hand over his thick, graying hair, avoiding eye contact. "You read the report. I was inebriated that night. I don't remember what happened."

"You could undergo hypnosis to recover your memory."

"Actually I've discussed it with Sloan and Zane. Stella was against it. Then she had the breakdown…"

Maybe she was too afraid of the answers they'd find. Either that he killed Lou Anne or *she* had.

"What about Stella? Do you think she might have killed Lou Anne?"

"Absolutely not." Jim shifted restlessly, toying with the snake braid on his hatband.

"Stella has always been weak, fragile. She wouldn't have the guts to murder anyone."

"Not even a woman who might steal her husband from her?" Cole's voice resonated with anger. "After all, Lou Anne wasn't your first indiscretion. Maybe she was just the one who sent Stella over the edge."

Jim shoved his hat back on his head. "I told you, she's not capable of murder."

"Anyone is capable of killing another person," Joey cut in. "Especially if they're driven to it."

Jim blasted Joey with an angry look, then started to stand.

"We're not finished, Mr. McKinney," Joey said.

He grunted. "I am."

Cole thumped his hand on the table. "One more question."

Turmoil registered in Jim's eyes. Did he think Cole was going to ask him something personal? Like why he'd never tried to see him, not even once during all the years he'd been so nearby?

"Whom else did you sleep with at the time?" Cole asked.

Jim's expression registered surprise, then confusion. "Why is that relevant?"

"I'm just trying to be thorough. If you, Stella, Leland or Donna didn't kill Lou Anne, perhaps one of your other lovers did? Maybe some woman who saw Lou Anne as a problem between the two of you?"

"If that's true, then why not kill Stella? She was my wife."

Cole nodded. "Maybe she thought she could convince you to leave your wife."

Jim stared at him for a long moment, emotions warring on his face. "I would never have left her," he said in a gravelly voice. "Every woman I slept with knew that."

Jim turned and walked away, leaving Cole's heart racing with fury and his message ringing in his head. Cole's mother had slept with him knowing he'd never leave his wife, but she'd loved him anyway.

COLE'S MOUTH tightened as he balled his hands into fists. Joey sensed he was at the end of his restraint, that he was about to chase down his father and punch him. She couldn't say that she blamed him.

The man had made no personal acknowledgment of his third son, no apology, no
I-love-you declarations.

Then again, she and Cole had been inter-
rogating him on possible murder charges.
And she supposed she had to admire the fact
that he had some decency and hadn't left his
wife, especially since Stella seemed so
fragile and needy.

"I need to get out of here," Cole said.

She reached out to comfort him, but he
shook his head. Pain radiated from his
features, making her heart swell with
unwanted emotions. She wanted to soothe
him and ease the pain.

Instead she started toward the exit. "I
guess we meet my father now."

He gave her an understanding look, then
his cell phone jangled. He answered it as they
stepped into the heat and walked to the sedan.

"Sergeant McKinney speaking."

She climbed in and fastened her seat belt
while he spoke in a low voice. When he
hung up, he started the car and the air conditioner, then shifted into gear and drove
from the parking lot.

"That was Deputy Burns. He's been reviewing Sarah Wallace's phone records."

"Did he find anything?"

"Just that Sarah called Jim McKinney before she died. Apparently Jim told him about the call, but he didn't speak to Sarah. He was gone and Stella took the call."

Joey tapped her nails on her thigh. "What if Stella thought Sarah wanted to pick up with Jim where her mother left off?"

"It's possible." Cole paused, twisting his mouth in thought. "Or Stella might have been worried that Sarah had the evidence to send either her or Jim to jail so she killed her."

Joey hesitated to bring up the painful subject, but they couldn't skirt it. "You're not buying Jim's story that Stella is too weak to commit murder?"

Cole shook his head. "I agree with you. Anyone is capable if they're pushed far enough. And Stella…had her reasons," he said tightly.

"Was there anything else?" Joey asked.

"They checked Donna's and Rosa's phone records as well. It seems Rosa was on the phone with her mother while Anna was strangled so that rules her out."

Joey's heart fluttered with shock. "You suspected Rosa of killing Sarah?"

He shrugged. "They've been looking into every conceivable angle, Joey. Apparently Donna has a bank account Sloan and Sheriff Matheson are investigating, so they examined all their phone records and are reviewing their financial statements."

Joey thumbed her fingers through her hair, raking the mass away from her cheek with a frown. She'd have to ask her mother about that account.

And Rosa was close to Donna and had been dedicated to her over the years. But Rosa had loved Justin more than life itself. She would have never been involved in a plot that might endanger him. Not loving, sweet Rosa who'd made sure Joey's clothes were clean and pressed for school, who'd made her enchiladas and baked chocolate fudge cookies for Justin. Rosa who had been a mother to Joey and Justin when Donna had her own affair with the bottle.

Nerves tightened every cell in her body as

Cole drove up the oak-lined driveway to her father's estate. Looking at his magnificent spread now, it was difficult to believe that Leland had ever been financially strapped.

But even if he had, it wouldn't have justified kidnapping his own son.

Cole parked, killed the engine, then turned to look at her. "Are you sure you're ready for this?"

"No." A nervous laugh escaped her, and Cole's mouth tilted into a smile.

"I like your honesty, Joey. That's rare these days."

She tensed. If she was totally honest, she'd admit to him how terrified she was that her parents might be guilty. That she wanted Jim McKinney to be the culprit.

Oddly Cole might understand. He must have mixed feelings about his father just as she had about her own.

They were very much alike in that manner. Both ignored, abandoned in some ways, yet putting up a tough front as if they didn't care about the outcome. But living with the stigma of being a murderer's child would only add to the pain they'd already been saddled with.

"We can come back later if you want."

How chivalrous of him to offer her a way out. "No, let's get this over with." Besides, she didn't intend to let him question Leland alone.

He opened the door and met her by the passenger side before she could climb out. As she led him up the brick walkway, he placed a hand to the small of her back, a gesture that felt comforting and intimate at the same time. She rang the doorbell, and he gave her a questioning look. This was supposed to be her home, but she had never felt at home here. Not like she had in the tiny house she remembered as a child, the one where her parents had still been happy.

A servant she didn't recognize answered the door. "Miss Hendricks, welcome. My name is Broderick, so let me know if you need anything. We've been wondering when you'd stop by."

"Is my father home?"

The balding, thin man dressed in a butler's uniform glanced suspiciously at Cole. "Yes. Who shall I say is here to visit?"

"Sergeant Cole McKinney, Texas Rangers."

Broderick nodded curtly, then gestured for them to follow him to her father's study, a massive room filled with leather couches, sleek cherry furniture, volumes of collector's books and journals and magazines filled with information for entrepreneurs and oil barons.

Broderick excused himself to retrieve her father, and Joey paced the office, feeling caged, and aching to run and escape the confrontation destined to ensue. Cole claimed a seat in one of the wing chairs, stretching his long legs out and looking at ease as he studied the room.

Five minutes later, an aproned woman appeared with a tray of cakes, tea and coffee. Joey's stomach revolted, but Cole accepted coffee. Her father strode in seconds later, wearing an expensive suit, his shoulders rigid, his gaze traveling from her to Cole in a condescending manner. He looked older and grayer, Joey noted, although he still dominated a room with his presence.

"Well, this is interesting," Leland said. "I didn't expect my first contact with you in years to be in the eyes of the Texas Rangers. Especially the bastard son of Jim McKinney."

Cole set his coffee cup down on the tray, the only indication that her father's comment angered him. But Joey knew differently. She was beginning to read the man and hated for him to have to endure such ridicule.

"Father, rudeness doesn't become you."

Her father snapped his head her way with a flare of indignation in his eyes. "I only spoke the truth."

"So, if you're into telling the truth these days, why don't you start with your part in the Wallace murders?" Cole asked in a voice steeped with barely controlled rage.

Leland picked up a cigar and rolled it between his fingers and thumb. "I've already given my statement to the sheriff and to the other Texas Rangers."

"We've read it," Joey said. "And you claim that you didn't have anything to do with Justin's kidnapping or murder?"

The agony that flashed into her father's eyes seemed so real and heart wrenching that Joey's throat closed. Her own guilt surfaced, causing pain to ricochet through her in waves that nearly made her double over.

Cole gave her an odd look, then piped up. "Did you?"

Leland sank into his desk chair and wiped at perspiration on his forehead. "I would never have hurt a child. There's not a day that goes by that I don't wish Justin had been found."

Missing his son didn't mean he hadn't orchestrated a plan that had gone awry. And he probably wanted Justin to be found to take suspicion off of himself.

Joey's resolve hardened. She remembered how convincing her father had been in court when he'd ruthlessly taken her and Justin from Donna. How he'd lied to have his affair.

"Dad, did you set up the kidnapping to get the insurance money?"

He shook his head. "How can you even ask me that, Joey?"

"How can I not?"

"Mr. Hendricks," Cole cut in. "Did you know about your wife's secret account?"

"No. If I had, I would have asked for help."

"Maybe you did and she refused you," Cole suggested.

Leland bristled. "That's ridiculous. I said I didn't know, and that's the truth."

Cole didn't look convinced. "We're aware that Lou Anne Wallace had an affair with Jim McKinney. Was he the only man she was seeing before her death?"

The question seemed to take him off guard. He rolled the cigar between his fingers again, then tapped it on the desk as if he wanted to light up but was trying to give up the habit.

"Dad?" Joey asked. "Was there another man…or men in Lou Anne's life?"

Confusion, anger, then hope sparkled on Leland's face as if he just realized the implication of the question. "Obviously there were, since there were two semen samples in her body when she died. But I don't know any names. And the police never pursued it. They just came after me."

Joey hadn't known about the second semen sample. She wondered if Cole had, if he'd intentionally kept the information from her.

Cole's phone jangled and he frowned,

checked the number, then stood. "It's Zane. I'd better take it."

Joey nodded, and her father watched Cole leave the room. Leland moved to the wall behind his desk, revealed a safe, methodically keyed in the combination, then opened the door. With a sigh, he removed a small, black worn book and handed it to Joey. "This belonged to Lou Anne. It was private. I…never showed it to the police."

"What is it?" Joey asked.

"Lou Anne's date book where she kept an account of all her…meetings. It might prove helpful."

Excitement raced through her veins. "Why didn't you show this to the police?

"I didn't want all of Lou Anne's indiscretions plastered over the papers. Her affair with McKinney was humiliating enough."

Cole's boots pounded on the marble floor, and she jammed the date book in her purse. She'd check it out first and see if it offered any information. Then she'd decide whether or not to show it to Cole. After all, it might prove to be nothing…

Then again, it might lead to Lou Anne and Sarah Wallace's killer.

And what about Justin—did the book contain information about her brother's kidnapping and murder?

IRRITATION CRAWLED through Cole as he drove Joey back to the Matheson Inn. Zane had phoned to inform him that the doctors had sedated Stella and were worried that she might permanently slip into a catatonic state. He had warned Cole not to visit her again.

Hell, he was sorry that Stella was so weak and ill. But she had made her choices years ago. And she might have killed Lou Anne or covered for her husband.

Jim had chosen her over Cole's mother who had loved him with all her heart. Barb Tyler had been a strong gutsy woman who'd deserved better.

His stomach rumbled, reminding him that they had missed lunch altogether. Storm clouds darkened the sky as they neared town, a town filled with secrets and deception.

A town where a murderer still lurked,

probably gloating over the fact that he—or she—had gotten away all this time.

He cut his gaze toward Joey. She had been quiet since climbing in the car and kept worrying her purse strap with her fingers. He knew the meeting with her father hadn't gone as she'd probably hoped.

"Do you want to stop for a late lunch, or early dinner?"

She bit down on her lip, and he reached up and touched her chin. "Joey?"

Behind him, a car raced up on his tail, and he jerked his gaze from Joey to the rearview mirror. He'd been mentally distracted and hadn't noticed the traffic, much less this car approaching so quickly.

He sped up slightly. The car sped up as well, then suddenly zoomed up close to his tail and swerved sideways. Seconds later, a loud popping sound echoed through the air, then a bullet pinged off the side of the car.

"Dammit. Hang on!"

Joey clenched the dashboard as he jerked the car sideways. "What was that?"

"Someone's shooting at us!"

He pressed the gas, and the sedan vaulted

forward. Joey turned to look at the car, but he swerved the opposite way and the sudden movement flung her against the car door. The gunfire pinged again, and he pulled to the left, but the right front tire popped. Damn. They were hit. Then the car raced up on his tail and slammed into them, sending them into a spin. Tires squealed and the scent of smoke spewed from the wheels. He cursed again. The shooter must have hit the gas tank.

A small hill sloped downward to a wooded area. He tried to maintain control, but lost it as the car spun and rolled toward the woods. Joey screamed, and he threw out his arm to shield her as glass exploded and the air bags deployed. The car rolled over, bounced, skidded, then slammed into a tree. Immediately the front of the car erupted into flames.

He yelled Joey's name. They had to get out before the car blew up completely!

Chapter Ten

Panic shot through Joey as the car skidded into the tree and fire burst from the hood. The air bag trapped her, and she was hanging upside down between it and the seat. The scent of smoke and gas permeated the air, raising her fear another notch. Her chest ached from the impact of the bag, and her arm from being thrown against the door, but she was alive.

Next to her, Cole grunted and swiped at the air bag. "Joey, are you all right?"

"Yeah. You?"

"Yes. But we have to get out of here fast. The car's going to blow any second."

"I know." She jiggled her seat belt trying to free it. "Cole, my seat belt is stuck!"

Cole ripped the air bag open with a pocketknife and shoved it away from her face, jerked off his own seat belt, then split the seat belt with the sharp blade, freeing her. She gripped the door handle and pushed her hand up to brace herself as her body slid down and her head hit the roof.

He hit the automatic button to roll down the windows but they didn't budge. "Dammit." Cole slammed his elbow into the window and the glass shattered. He chipped away the remaining jagged edges with the knife, then turned to her. "Come on. We have to crawl out."

He shoved his broad shoulders through, and dove onto the ground while Joey crawled to the driver's side. She grabbed her purse and he pulled her through the opening headfirst. Her heart pounded at the sight of the flames shooting from the front of the car. Heat suffused her face, and the smell of gasoline filled her nostrils as she landed on top of Cole. He caught her, and they rolled sideways on the ground, then he dragged her toward a clearing away from the sedan. A fraction of a second later, the car exploded with a thunderous roar and bright orange flames colored the gray sky, smoke billowing in a thick cloud.

Joey heaved for a breath as Cole leaned against a tree. She searched the road and woods for the shooter or another car, and saw Cole doing the same, but the driver had left them to die.

The thought sent another shudder through her, and she realized how close they'd come to death.

Cole turned her to face him. "Are you hurt?"

She shook her head, but her shoulder and chest ached. She might have cracked a rib or two and she'd have more bruises. His hand was bleeding from the broken glass, his face covered with sweat and dusted with soot.

Their gazes met, anger and fear pumping adrenaline through her. She saw the same emotions mirrored in his eyes as he yanked her into his arms and held her.

"God, Joey," Cole said in a gruff voice. "That was close."

"I know." She leaned into his strength, unable to remember the last time she'd let someone support her. But she couldn't resist now.

"Did you see anything?" she whispered.

He rested his head on top of hers. "No, just a dark car. I couldn't even get the make."

Joey clung to his arms and pressed her face into his warmth. Today they had confronted Stella, Jim McKinney and her father. Had one of their own family members tried to have them killed? It was hard to believe they might be so evil….

The date book in her purse felt heavy, reminding her that it might hold a clue as to Lou Anne's killer. She had to study it tonight and see if it offered answers.

Cole stroked her back while the car continued to burn. Fire hissed and popped, crackling. Heat seared her skin, the flames painting lines of orange and red across Cole's strong face.

Cole removed his cell phone and punched in a number. "Zane, it's Cole. Someone just tried to kill me and Joey." He paused. "A dark car. Gunshots fired at us. The car sideswiped us and sent us into a spin. We need a fire truck and crime team out here now."

Joey closed her eyes. All she wanted to do was retreat to the inn and bury herself in

Cole's arms. Kiss him and have him hold her all night and help her forget that her own family might be out to destroy her.

WITHIN MINUTES, sirens wailed and bright lights flickered through the sky as the fire truck screeched to a stop. Zane raced up on the heels of the fire truck, a crime scene unit van following, one of the deputies vaulting out with him. Unfortunately Dennison was in tow as well, shooting photos as he approached.

"Get the crime scene area roped off immediately!" Zane ordered. "And keep Dennison out!"

The deputy jumped into motion, as did the crime unit and firemen.

Zane took one look at the inferno that had been Cole's Rangers-issued car and anger blazed in his eyes. "Are you guys all right?"

"Just bruised and scratched," Cole said. "I can't believe the guy escaped."

Zane spun on Dennison. "Get the hell out of here!"

"You'd be better off cooperating," Dennison sputtered as he snapped a shot of

Zane. "Your antagonism only makes you look guilty of conspiracy to cover up a crime."

Zane froze, a lethal look in his eyes. Cole felt the same rage burn within him, and grappled for control.

Joey stepped forward, irritation on her face, but her voice remained calm. "I'll take care of him." She pulled Dennison to the side, gave him a short version of what had happened, then they spoke in hushed tones.

"What did you see?" Zane asked.

Cole kept an eye on them while he spoke to Zane. He didn't like the fact that Dennison was one step behind them.

"Nothing much. The car raced up behind me, but I couldn't get the model or see the driver."

"I'll have the crime techs look for tire marks," Zane said.

"Dammit, you won't be able to retrieve paint samples from where the other car hit us off of that charred mess," Cole said in disgust.

Zane went to confer with the crime unit while Dennison headed to his van, looking vaguely satisfied.

"How'd you manage that?" Cole asked.

"I promised to share the crime report when the guys are finished."

Cole grunted, still battling the rage inside him as the firemen extinguished the blaze, and the paramedics bandaged his wrist and examined Joey for injuries. She admitted to bruised ribs from the air bag's force and a sore arm, and the paramedic insisted on taking her to the hospital for X-rays. She protested but Cole spoke up.

"Please, Joey. We want to document any injuries so when we catch this SOB we can use it in court to nail him."

Her face looked strained but she conceded. She obviously wanted the shooter to pay for what he'd done as much as he did.

"Once I finish here, I'll meet up with you at the hospital," he said.

Joey nodded and climbed into the ambulance with a frown. An odd pang hit him at seeing her in the ambulance, and he realized that he had the urge to go with her.

Just a protective instinct, he assured himself. Nothing more. He wasn't going to *miss* her. He was simply worried about her safety.

For the next hour and a half, he worked with Zane to oversee the crime unit and search for any signs of tire marks or that the car might have stopped and the shooter might have climbed out, but they found nothing. They had to wait until the fire died and cooled to search for the bullet casings, or see if one had lodged in the tire.

"Where did you go after you left the hospital?" Zane asked.

Cole shrugged. "We paid Leland Hendricks a visit."

Zane's brows shot up at that. "And?"

"He denied killing Lou Anne and Sarah Wallace just as he did before."

"Did he offer any new information?"

Cole shook his head. "No. If he's guilty, he's not going to confess." Not unless they found some hard evidence against him. "But he confirmed that Lou Anne had an affair with another man. Someone besides Jim. He didn't give us a name, though."

Zane rammed a hand through his hair. "That's right. There were two semen samples. That's one of the points the lawyer used to get Dad off back then."

"Joey and I will see if we can find out who it was."

Zane nodded. "Let me know if you do. By the way, Leland drives a dark Cadillac. Do you think he could have followed you and Joey?"

Cole's stomach twitched. He didn't want to think Leland would hurt his own daughter, but he didn't trust the man. "I don't know. It seems too risky a move for a hotshot like him to do himself."

"You're probably right. Leland's style would be to hire someone."

"Like the guy who attacked Joey in her room?"

Zane nodded.

Cole cleared his throat as Zane started to walk off. "Zane, I…I'm sorry about your mother."

Zane's gaze bore into his as if searching for an underlying meaning. Finally he seemed to realize Cole's sincerity, and gave a curt nod. "Thanks. Come on and I'll give you a ride to the hospital to pick up Joey."

Cole followed him, an odd feeling settling in his gut. He had no idea why he'd apologized about Stella McKinney. He'd hated the entire family for years. Had known that Stella hated him. And her reaction proved that she blamed him for her problems, that he was an embarrassment to the entire family. That she'd never accept him.

And Jim McKinney seemed cowed by her so he would never accept Cole, either.

But he'd seen the pain in Zane's and Sloan's eyes when Stella had collapsed, and remembered taking care of his own mother when she'd become ill. How helpless he'd felt. How angry at the fates. And he'd felt some small connection with his half brothers.

Still, the distance between them was too long a bridge to cross. He would never fit in with the McKinneys. The way Jim had treated him earlier had driven that fact home with bone-jarring clarity.

When the investigation ended, he would return to his life, and the McKinneys would never be a part of it.

JOEY PACED the hospital waiting room, anxious for Cole to arrive. She hated hospitals, always had. But she hated being in the dark even more. Anger stirred inside her. If someone wanted to scare her off, they'd gone about it the wrong way. Her Taurus personality kicked in, her resolve to finish the investigation hardening.

The sliding doors squeaked open and Cole rushed in. "Sorry it took me so long. Zane and I decided to run by and get me another car so I'd have transportation. Didn't think you'd be up for a ride on the Harley."

"I'd love to ride on it sometime," Joey said. "But it's probably not the safest mode of travel when a killer is shooting at us. Did you find any evidence?"

"No, but hopefully the crime unit will retrieve the bullet casing. Are you ready?"

"Definitely." She clutched her purse over her shoulder, determined not to lose the date book inside.

Ironic that she was putting her life on the line to help a woman who had stolen her father from her mother and ruined her life.

"Are you all right?" Cole tipped her chin up with his thumb. "You look pale, Joey. Do you need to stay overnight?"

"No," she said. "I want to go back to the inn with you."

His breath hissed out, tension vibrating between them. "Then let's go. We'll stop and grab dinner on the way."

Joey tried to relax in the seat as he drove to a steak house on the outskirts of Justice.

At least no one in town would know them here, and they could have a reprieve from the killer and the nosy press. Joey ordered a filet, baked potato and wine. Cole ordered a T-bone, onion rings and beer, and the two of them ate like they hadn't seen food in days.

"What did the doctor say?" Cole asked.

Cole attacked his meal like he did everything else—with strength of purpose. He'd even managed a small moan at the first bite.

She found herself wondering if he would moan like that when they made love. And if he would attack her with the same fervor, savor each bite...

His gaze met hers, and a spark of electricity rippled between them that was so strong Joey shivered. "Joey?"

"Bruises, but no broken bones," she whispered.

"Good." He wrapped his hand around the

beer bottle, and she suddenly had an image of him wrapping those long fingers around her. Stroking her face, her breasts, her belly, then dipping lower and sliding inside her. She shifted in the seat, a shot of fire igniting her thighs.

He ran a finger over her hand, stroking softly, his gaze latching onto hers as if he felt the chemistry, too. "You're tired?"

"Today has been…stressful." All she wanted to do was to crawl into his bed. His arms. Taste his kiss and feel him moan her name against her neck.

He nodded. "Are you ready to go?"

"Yes." She swirled her wine in the glass, then took the last sip and rolled it on her tongue. She could almost taste him. Wanted to taste him. All of him. "Definitely."

His eyes turned a smoky-gray. Then he motioned for the waitress and asked for the bill. A heartbeat later, they slipped back in the car. The silence that stretched between them should have been awkward. Instead it was filled with excited anticipation. Today had been hell for both of them. Confronting parents they hadn't seen in years. Parents who had hurt them. And then the shooting and wreck, and the car exploding.

Tonight they deserved to assuage the pain and remember that they were both alive, that circumstances had thrown them together.

That and the raw sexual tension brimming between them. A tension she wanted to absolve while she was in his arms, naked and quaking with his delicious touches.

She tried to remember the reasons that sleeping with Cole was a bad idea as he parked and they walked into the inn. But the ache in her body and soul overrode any reservations, and by the time they reached her room, she unlocked the door and dragged him inside.

COLE SILENTLY GROANED as Joey pulled him into her room. During dinner, his mind had taken an interesting ride into fantasyland. A land where Joey's endless legs were wrapped around his body, and he was thrusting inside her like a wild man.

He knew enough about police work and near-death experiences to realize that they were both pumped from an adrenaline high.

But a deeper need had driven him to forget his resolve.

He hadn't been able to stop thinking about her when she'd left him at the crime scene. And when he'd seen her waiting for him at the hospital, his hands had moved of their own volition. He had to touch her. To feel her next to him tonight. To know that she was alive, and that tomorrow they would both wake to see the dawn.

Feeling like a fool for thinking such nonsense, he paused in the doorway, but Joey caught him by the collar and began to remove his tie. His throat convulsed, and he whispered her name in a ragged tone that sounded far away, as if it had come from a stranger.

"Cole, please. I…need to touch you."

"I know," he said gruffly. A sultry look grazed her eyes, and he succumbed to the yearning and threaded his fingers through her hair. God, it felt more heavenly than he'd imagined. Like fine gold silk across his belly.

What would it feel like across his bare belly? he wondered.

He had to know.

He cupped her face in his hands and

sighed with the knowledge that he'd never met a woman like Joey Hendricks. He probably never would again.

"Joey, tonight—"

"No promises," she whispered. "It's just tonight."

Tonight he could live with. Promises that he couldn't keep he would never make.

But loving her was something he could do. So he let her remove his shirt. The sound of the buttons popping sent a bolt of white-hot lust through him. And when she stood on tiptoe to kiss him, and he lowered his head and claimed her mouth with his own, his sex hardened and pushed against his fly, aching for the sweet haven her body offered.

She parted her lips and took his tongue inside, then suckled him until he thought his body would explode. He walked her backward toward the bed and his fingers moved to her tank top, then he slid his hands down and lifted it over her head. His heart pounding, he trailed kisses down her neck and his hands cupped her breasts. This time she wore a lavender bra that was so lacy her nipples budded through the thin barrier, begging for his taste. He closed his lips around one turgid peak and pulled it into his mouth, licking and sucking the tip.

She moaned and gripped his arms to hold herself upright, then threw her head back in wild abandon. Joey Hendricks was a force to be reckoned with. Unlike any other woman he'd ever been with. Or loved.

Loved?

No, loved physically. Not emotionally. Cole couldn't let that happen....

She stroked his arm, his chest, then moved her hand lower to cup him, and his body told his brain to shut up.

He laved her other breast with his tongue while his hand inched to her waist, and he ripped her skirt down her thighs. Joey kicked off the garment, revealing a lavender thong that took his breath away. The sprinkling of blond curls at the juncture of her thighs made his mouth water for her sweet taste. He pushed her back onto the bed and stripped her underwear, then stepped back and drank in the sight of her naked body stretched out on the bed. She was an angel in a devil's sultry body, a woman who stole the air from his lungs.

He teased her legs apart with his hands, then lowered his mouth, tracing his tongue along her feminine folds, savoring the heart of her as she writhed beneath him.

"Cole?"

He ignored her tortured plea and continued his ministrations, his body thrumming with raw hunger. Her hips lifted off the mattress, and she clutched the sheets, twisting them in her hands as she cried out his name.

Sweat beaded along his spine as he finished lapping her up, then removed his jeans. His sex bulged, aching to be inside her, to claim her as his own.

But his cell phone rang, a shrill sound that sliced the air and made him pause.

"Cole, don't answer it," Joey whispered.

The shiny metal of his badge twinkled in the sliver of the moonlight, and Cole's instincts and training drove him to reach for the phone. He was a Ranger first, a man second. He always would be. And no woman had ever changed that, or ever would.

Making love to her would have to wait.

He recognized Zane's number, rose and moved to the window and looked out into the dark street. "Sergeant Cole McKinney."

"Cole, Zane. Forensics retrieved the bullet from the car you were driving. Another .38."

"Just like the casing I found in the woods."

"Exactly. And Cole…Donna had a .38 that we confiscated already. She might have bought another."

Cole glanced at Joey lying naked in the bed beneath the sheet, and worry slammed into him. "Anything else?"

"Sloan and Carley have been checking into Donna's bank accounts. For the past ten years, Donna has been purchasing a cashier's check for $1,000 a month."

Cole angled himself away from Joey. He couldn't stare at her sultry body and those still-aroused eyes while he discussed her mother as a suspect. "You think it was blackmail money?"

"It's possible. Maybe someone found out that she killed Lou Anne and she's been paying for their silence."

Unease tickled Cole's neck. How would Joey react to that news?

"Listen, since Joey seems to trust you, maybe you could find out what she knows about the money."

Cole's stomach knotted. "I don't think she knows anything. She's been estranged from her family for years."

Zane grunted. "Maybe that's because she knows they're guilty. Did you ever think that she might be here to sabotage the investigation? That she might be cozying up to you to keep tabs on us and our case against her parents?"

A frisson of unease seized Cole. He had considered that possibility, but his logic had disintegrated when he looked at those mile-long legs and those irresistible eyes. Eyes that mesmerized a man and made his mind turn toward lust and fantasies of long, hot nights doing nothing but riding her.

Damn. He had lost his objectivity.

"Cole?"

Zane wanted him to use Joey. He had come here to prove that he deserved to wear the Ranger badge as much as his half brothers did. Here was his chance.

"Sure, I'll let you know what I find out."

He hung up, and reached for his jeans. No way he could finish their lovemaking, though, not with the sour taste of what he had to do burning his stomach.

Joey sat up, the sheet riding down to reveal those luscious breasts. Breasts that he had teased and loved only a few moments ago. She indicated the bed, inviting him back, her vulnerable but teasing look so enticing he almost relented and crawled on top of her.

Joey trusted him. But he was going to break that trust.

"Cole?"

"It's late," he said in a gruff voice.

"Who was that on the phone?"

"Zane."

"What did he say?"

Cole shrugged. "They dug the bullet from the car. It came from a .38."

She sighed and twisted the covers over her. "Half the state of Texas owns a .38. Heck, even I do."

He nodded. He ached to go to her and climb back in bed. To thrust himself inside her.

But even though everyone in town knew

him to be a bastard, he couldn't sleep with her tonight, not knowing that she might be using him. Or that he had to use her, and that he might have to arrest her mother tomorrow.

Chapter Eleven

Joey's body still quivered with the aftermath of her orgasm. For tonight, she'd wanted to forget the investigation and bury herself in Cole's arms. Already he was the best lover she'd ever experienced. And they hadn't completely finished…

Emotions mingled with the elation of her physical response as she watched him pull on his jeans. His body was magnificent. Bulging defined pecs and broad shoulders. Then that washboard stomach and those muscular thighs. Even his butt was finely sculpted…and his sex. Heavens. She wanted to feel his thick, long length inside her.

Desire heated her body while her chest swelled with another sensation. A tug of affection. Emotions that she had no business feeling for the Texas Ranger. Emotions that scared her to death.

Governor Grange expected her to be the rational, objective one in this case. And how could she do that if her heart turned to mush over one of the McKinney men?

She glanced at her purse and remembered the little black book that had belonged to Lou Anne and itched to check out the contents. Surely her father wouldn't have handed it over to her if it implicated him. But it might contain damning information on Cole's father.

Granted, Cole pretended he didn't care about the man, but deep down she sensed he wanted some kind of gesture from Jim to show that he cared for him. It was only human nature to crave a parent's love.

She certainly had. Heck, she'd realized long ago that her ambition and desire to prove herself in business, her climb to the governor's office, had been an attempt to make her parents proud. Not that they'd ever congratulated her or noticed…

Why had Cole decided to leave her bed? Why wasn't he returning to finish what they'd started?

His blue eyes turned smoky as he grabbed his shirt. Still his eyes skated over her, and hunger burned in his gaze. A tingle of anxiety stole into her euphoria. "Cole? What else did Zane say? Something upset you."

He moved toward her, then sat down on the side of the bed and threaded his fingers into her hair. His touch melted her into a puddle of need again, blatant hunger humming through her bloodstream. "Cole?"

"Sloan and Sheriff Matheson discovered that Donna was buying a cashier's check for $1,000 every month for the past few years."

Joey gasped.

"She hasn't been sending you the money?"

Suddenly feeling cold and exposed, she covered her breasts. "No."

"Do you know what she's doing with the money?"

"I have no idea. I told you Donna and I hadn't spoken in years." Her stomach twisted as she realized the implication. "You think it's blackmail money?"

He shrugged. "I don't know. But we have to find out."

Joey's throat clogged with fear.

He leaned forward and placed a gentle kiss on her forehead. The tender gesture confused her even more.

"Get some rest. We'll look into it tomorrow."

She grabbed his arm to keep him from leaving. "But, Cole?" She rubbed a hand over his thigh, stroked him through his jeans. "I want you to be satisfied."

A grin inched up the corner of his mouth. "Honey, I had a great time." He kissed her again for emphasis, and she tasted herself on his lips. Her cheeks flamed red when he pulled away.

"Cole—"

"Shh." He pressed a finger to her lips. "Let me do the right thing here, Joey."

She didn't quite know what he meant, but she had a feeling he thought sex would interfere with the case. She should thank him for being a gentleman. For stopping her before she gave herself to him completely.

And making love to him just might tempt her to tear down the guardrail protecting her heart.

He walked to the door, turned and seared her with one last hungry look, then closed the door.

But his last comment worried her. Donna had been withdrawing money each month for the past few years. Was she paying off a blackmailer?

IT TOOK EVERY OUNCE of restraint Cole possessed to leave Joey's bedroom. Knowing that she still wanted him drove him insane with desire. Dammit, how had she gotten into his head so quickly?

He growled in frustration. He had done the right thing by walking out. His father had allowed his libido to guide his decisions and look where he'd ended up. If Joey discovered that Zane wanted him to use her, she'd be furious.

Just as he would be if he found out she was using him.

He had to accept the fact that it was possible. That she might not be sharing everything she knew about her family.

Too antsy to sleep, he phoned forensics for a progress report. A detective named

Simmons answered. Cole had worked with him on prior cases and trusted him.

"We finally got a lead on the fingerprint on the bullet retrieved in the woods. Belongs to a man named Hector Elvarez."

"Do you know where I can find him?"

"He was working on a ranch in Mineral Wells. The Lucky S."

The Lucky S? Hmm. Mineral Wells, about thirty, forty miles from Justice. And not far from Dallas where Donna bought her cashier's checks each month.

"I'll pay him a visit in the morning. See who hired him to shoot at Sheriff Matheson," Cole said. "My guess is he's the same guy who also shot at us."

An uneasy feeling snaked through him. Donna was looking more and more guilty.

If she was covering up for murder, and had hired this guy to shoot at them, then tough girl aside, Joey would be devastated.

JOEY YANKED on a nightshirt. The thought of her mother being a murderer and blackmailing someone to hide her guilt shattered her night of euphoric bliss.

Panic washed over, but she tamped it down, grabbed her purse and removed Lou Anne's little black book.

Maybe Sloan and Cole were wrong. Maybe she'd find something inside to exonerate her parents.

She flipped on the lamp, propped herself against the mound of feather pillows and began to flip through the pages. As expected, she discovered various dates where Lou Anne had rendezvoused with Jim McKinney. The last one on the day she'd died.

Had Leland not cheated on her mother, Joey might have felt sorry for him. But she had adopted her mother's bitterness over his infidelities. Not only had he destroyed their family and Donna, he had taken her and Justin from the only home they'd ever known to be raised by servants.

She flipped back to the beginning, then studied each page more thoroughly. The name, Sly Jones, drew her eye. She tried to recall who he was, then realized he had been her mother's tax attorney. If she remembered correctly, he died a few years back. She searched through several more pages, then gasped.

No. It couldn't be.

Another man's name that she recognized. She turned several more pages and found his name again. Notations to meet at a hotel in Dallas.

Anger mounted on top of shock as she realized that Lou Anne's other lover had been Clayton Grange.

The current governor of Texas.

The man who'd sent her here to handle the media.

She fell back against the covers in stunned silence, her stomach convulsing. Governor Grange had been a young man then, an up-and-comer in politics. A man from a prominent family. A man who helped handle the investigation of her brother's disappearance and Lou Anne's murder. And he had been married at the time, a newlywed. The last thing he would have wanted was a scandal.

Lou Anne had been disgusted with Leland's financial situation. Had she sought out the governor? Seduced him? Maybe threatened to expose their affair if he didn't leave his wife for her? Or maybe she'd wanted money to keep quiet?

Could Governor Grange have killed Lou Anne to save his reputation?

And if he had, would he expect her to cover for him?

BETWEEN HIS BODY yearning for a night with Joey, his mind replaying various scenarios about the case and his guilt over possibly using the only woman he'd been attracted to in ages, Cole suffered a sleepless night. He took a cold shower the next morning, then dressed in his jeans, white shirt, standard tie and Stetson and pinned on his badge, reminding himself that his job was all that mattered. Being a Ranger was what he lived for. He had no family, no ties, and he didn't need them. They would interfere with his head when he needed to focus. The sooner he cracked and closed this case, the sooner he could leave town and be done with the McKinneys. They'd made it clear they didn't want him here.

And Cole McKinney didn't hang around where he wasn't wanted.

Bracing himself for the sight of the blond beauty who'd haunted his dreams all night, he knocked on her door. She answered, already dressed. A pale blue sundress show-cased her sinful legs, and her long hair swung free making him itch to sink his fingers into the silky tresses.

"Good morning, Cole."

Her smile seemed a little too bright and fake. "Is it?"

She shrugged. "I don't know yet. But let's go talk to my mother."

He nodded. He understood her trepidation. He wasn't exactly looking forward to the confrontation, either. Which disturbed him.

He shouldn't care about an interview or how it might affect Joey.

Early morning sunshine beat down on them as they walked to the diner, drilling home the fact that he was actually worried about her. The sound of hushed voices of early morning locals filtered through the strained silence as they entered the diner. Two elderly ladies sipped coffee at a table near the door and a family with four kids fought over the pancake syrup.

The bell tinkled, announcing their arrival and Donna glanced up from the counter. A hesitant smile lit her eyes as if she was happy to see her daughter but wondered why she was with the likes of a bastard like him. Rosa flitted over to Joey and hugged her.

"Joey, are you okay? I heard about the accident."

Her thick accent slowed her down, but Joey seemed unfazed. "Yes, I'm okay."

Rosa's eyebrows furrowed in concern as she examined Joey for injuries. "I saw on news where you in accident." She lapsed into several sentences of heated Spanish that Cole tried to discern. But she was so upset he couldn't follow. "Are you hurt?"

"No, Rosa, I'm fine." She smiled and squeezed Rosa's hands. "Don't worry."

Rosa clucked, shaking her head from side to side. "It is too dangerous for you here askin' questions. Please, my little bebé, leave things alone."

"Rosa, everything will be fine." Joey waved off her concern and slid into a booth. "Now, we want some breakfast, then I need to speak to my mother."

Rosa's eyes darkened. "*Sí.* I get you breakfast. Omelet or empanadas?"

"Coffee and empanadas would be great," Joey said. "I've missed your cooking."

Rosa smiled although tears glittered in her eyes as she scribbled Cole's order and bustled to the kitchen.

Donna appeared at the register to handle several customers and watched them warily as Joey and Cole ate. When they'd both finished their second cup of coffee, Joey stood. "It's time."

Cole nodded, threw some money on the table, then followed her to the counter.

"Donna, we need to talk," Joey said matter-of-factly.

Donna appeared calm as she finished stacking the bills by the register. "All right. Let's go to my office."

Joey and Cole followed, the air between them fraught with tension. When they reached her office, Donna seated herself in her desk chair, crossed her legs and gestured for them to sit in the two adjacent chairs. "To what do I owe this honor?"

Cole had read that Leland was a hothead under pressure and Donna the calm one. She was proving that correct. At least for now.

"Mother, it's come to our attention that you've been going to Dallas and buying a cashier's check each month for $1,000." Joey fisted her hands in her lap. "What is the money for?"

Donna ran a finger along the edge of her desk, seemingly undisturbed by Joey's bluntness. "I donate it to a children's home, a charity," she said in a low voice. When she looked up at Joey, a well of anguish filled her eyes. "I know it won't bring back your brother, but I wanted to do something in honor of Justin."

Cole chewed the inside of his cheek, studying her while Joey's expression softened. "That's a nice gesture, Donna. Really."

Cole shuffled his boots, kicking the toe against the edge of the chair. Was Donna telling the truth? "What's the name of the charity?"

"It goes through a church in Dallas. St. Francis." Donna scribbled the name and address of the Catholic church on a notepad. "There, check it out yourself."

Cole nodded. He intended to do just that.

Donna excused herself to freshen up, dismissing them.

Outside the door, Rosa cornered Joey and pulled her to the side.

"Joey, I see your mama. She upset. Crying. Said you askin' questions?"

"Yes, Rosa. The sheriff found out about Donna purchasing a cashier's check each month. They thought she might be paying off a blackmailer to keep quiet."

Rosa's coffee-colored skin paled slightly. "Listen to me, little one. I help raise you, and I know you care about your mama. Please don't keep askin' questions. You are only hurtin' your mama more, and endangering yourself."

Joey clutched Rosa's arm. "Don't worry about me, Rosa. I'll be fine. Maybe I'll even find evidence that will clear Donna once and for all."

Rosa shook her head. "Leave it alone, Joey, *sí?* Please, for Rosa."

Joey hugged her. "I promise I'll be careful."

Cole frowned at the glint of worry in Rosa's eyes. Did she know more than she'd told them? Was she covering for Donna and trying to dissuade Joey because she knew Donna was guilty?

JOEY DESPERATELY wanted to believe Donna. And she had to talk to the governor. She'd really prefer a personal meeting, but she didn't know how to escape Cole without making him suspicious, so she'd called and left a message. "Where to now?" she asked as they climbed in the sedan.

"I talked to forensics last night. They traced the bullet slug I found in the woods near the inn to a man named Hector Elvarez."

"The bullet fired at Sheriff Matheson?"

"Yes. Elvarez works at a ranch near Mineral Wells. I thought we'd ride out there and talk to him."

"Finally a real lead." Joey's heart raced with adrenaline. "But why would Elvarez want to kill the sheriff?"

"He was probably a hired gun."

Joey nodded and stared at the landscape as they drove toward Mineral Wells. Maybe this man would give them answers. But she still had to question Governor Grange. She'd worked for him for four years now, had thought his marriage proof that happily-ever-after existed. That there was a man or two in the world who could be faithful.

Now that notion and her image of him were crushed. She admired the governor's political views, his fairness in dealing with issues and his staff, his concern for the state. And he'd given her a chance even though her family name preceded her.

But had he hired her in order to keep tabs on how much she knew about the past?

And how would the governor's supporters feel if they knew he had committed adultery when he spouted old-time family values as part of his campaign?

She glanced at Cole's firmly set jaw. They had a half hour drive, and she wanted to know more about him. "What was it like for you growing up?"

A flash of anger shadowed his blue eyes. Anger that didn't quite mask the pain.

"I liked ranch life," he said simply.

He was avoiding the real question. She sighed and rubbed his arm. "Did your father ever try to see you?"

He scraped his hand through his hair. "No. I...never met him or my half brothers until I came to Justice."

"Tell me about your mother."

His expression softened slightly. "She had a great smile. Worked hard. Did the best she could for us."

"Jim didn't provide financial support?"

"My mother told me once that he offered her money, but she didn't intend to be treated like a kept woman." He made a sarcastic sound. "I know people in Justice thought she was a home wrecker, but she loved Jim McKinney." His hands tightened around the steering wheel. "I never understood that. How she could love him when he didn't take care of her or his own son?"

"We don't choose the people we fall in love with, Cole," Joey said softly. "Sometimes it just happens." She lay her hand over his and he stiffened. She wondered if she'd said too much. Sounded as if she might be declaring her love when he didn't want to hear it.

She was smart enough to realize that this was the wrong time for her to get involved with anyone, too. But she couldn't deny how drawn she felt to Cole, how much she admired him for being a self-made man.

"What happened to your mother, Cole?"

"She had a heart attack." He sighed. "She was only forty at the time, but I guess the stress and hard work were too much for her."

She trailed her fingers through the scruffy ends of his dark hair where it brushed his collar. Maybe his mother had died of heartache. "How old were you?"

He clenched his jaw. "Fifteen. I stayed on at the ranch where she worked as a cook. Tried the rodeo circuit but I was getting into trouble, then Clete, the owner of the ranch, set me straight. Later I joined the service and they did the rest."

"That must have been hard, going on without your mother."

He slanted her a sideways glance. "You didn't exactly have a perfect childhood, Joey. Your parents' divorce, then your brother's kidnapping…"

He let the sentence trail off and she gulped back tears. "No, it wasn't easy. I hated Leland for cheating on my mother. Hated him for breaking up our family and then taking me and Justin from Mother."

"Weren't you old enough to choose who you wanted to live with?"

She dropped her hand to her side, and he twined their fingers together. "Yes," she said through a blur of emotions. "But I took care of Justin. He would have been lost if I hadn't gone with him. He loved Rosa, but he hated Daddy's housekeeper, and he cried for Mother at night." She tried to keep the memories of the fire at bay, but they crashed into her consciousness anyway.

"You were at Donna's the night Justin was kidnapped?"

Joey nodded, seeing her mother's panicked look in her mind. "It was one of the rare occasions when Leland allowed it." She hesitated. "Later, after the kidnapping and murder charges were brought up, I wondered if revenge was the reason he'd allowed us to stay there. So it would look like Donna was incompetent, and he'd have an alibi."

"How did he react to the fire? Did he seem shocked?"

"That's just it," Joey said, still haunted by doubt. "He did act shocked and devastated. It was the only instance where I'd seen my father cry. And later, when Justin was deemed dead, he seemed withdrawn. Of course, just like in the divorce, they both blamed each other." And Joey had never stopped blaming herself.

They reached a wooden cross post sign with the Lucky S painted in red and black, and Cole steered the car down the driveway. Joey glanced across the acreage noting the beef cattle and horses grazing in the pastureland. The scenery was beautiful and peaceful, although the lush green hillside and grazing cows proved it was a working cattle ranch.

Cole maneuvered down the dirt driveway, then parked at a two-story farmhouse that looked inviting. To the right, sat two barns and a stable with pen and corrals. A couple of ranch hands were training cutter horses in the corral. Another in a dusty cowboy hat groomed a beautiful smoky-colored mare.

Cole parked and cut the engine while Joey surveyed the front of the stable where a young man wearing a white Stetson and jeans cantered up on a tall black stallion. He rode with such skill and confidence that he must have grown up on horses. Just like Donna.

He noticed their car, jumped off the horse and called for one of the other hands. "Rodney, we have company. See that Dante is groomed while I find out who they are."

Sunlight glinted off his black hat as he approached, nearly blinding Joey as she climbed from the car. The young man was probably around seventeen. His confident swagger reminded her of someone, but she couldn't quite pinpoint whom.

Then he removed his Stetson and her breath caught in her chest. He had Donna's eyes. Her coloring. Her chin.

She staggered slightly and gripped the wooden pen rail to steady herself as the realization kicked in. This boy might be her missing brother, Justin.

Or was she imagining things because she desperately wanted him to be alive?

Chapter Twelve

Cole heard Joey's gasp and frowned. She leaned against the rail, her face pale in spite of the sun blazing a fiery path across her skin.

"What's wrong?" he asked.

"Look at him, Cole. He…he has Donna's eyes."

Cole studied the young man for similarities to indicate she was right.

"I can't believe it," Joey said in a choked whisper. "It has to be him. Justin. He's really alive."

Cole placed a hand over hers as he mentally analyzed the situation. "Joey, be careful. If this is Justin, and he was abducted and adopted by strangers, he may not be aware of what happened to him."

She pressed a hand to her mouth, but

nodded in understanding. Although she gripped the rail tighter as if she had to restrain herself from leaping forward and pulling the boy into a hug.

"Howdy, folks. What can I do for you?"

"My name is Sergeant Cole McKinney, Texas Rangers." Cole extended his hand, and the boy shook it firmly. "And this is Joey Hendricks, she's a special investigator for the governor."

Apparently impressed, the young man's eyes lit up with interest. How would he feel if it turned out that Joey was his sister?

"Caleb Sangston. Pleased to meet you."

"Caleb, is this your home?" Cole asked.

"Yeah. Well, the spread belongs to Dad."

Joey flinched slightly, and Cole rubbed her back to calm her. "Is your father here?"

Caleb nodded. "Sure. Come on. I'll show you in." He kicked dirt and grass from his boots as he entered the farmhouse, and Cole and Joey followed. She was beginning to pull herself together, but excitement and other emotions glittered in her eyes.

"Dad!" Caleb shouted. "We've got company."

A graying man in jeans, a Western shirt

and boots stood at an old-fashioned sink with a mug of coffee in his beefy hand. When he noted Cole's badge, he stiffened.

Caleb gestured toward them. "Dad, this is Sergeant McKinney of the Texas Rangers. And Joey Hendricks. She works for the governor's office."

"Walter Sangston." The man wiped his work roughened hands on a gingham towel, then waved toward the primitive pine table nicked from use and age, and they sat down. "I know who she is." He gave Joey a small smile. "I figured you'd show up here eventually."

Joey curled her fingers around the table edge. "Really?"

"Yeah." He offered them coffee but Cole declined. Joey accepted some ice water, though, and chugged it down.

"Mr. Sangston," Cole said. "We have some questions to ask you."

Sangston nodded warily. Caleb poured himself a glass of iced tea, then leaned against the sink, his interest obviously piqued.

"Caleb," Sangston started. "Maybe you'd better wait outside."

"Actually he should probably stay," Cole suggested.

Sangston's lips thinned, but then a resigned look fell across his craggy features. "All right."

Once again taking the lead, Cole explained about their investigation. "We traced a bullet casing from the woods where Sheriff Matheson was shot to a ranch hand who works for you."

Sangston's gray eyebrows shot up. "One of mine?"

"Yes, a man named Hector Elvarez."

"Hector hasn't worked here in a couple of months," Sangston said quickly.

Cole glanced at Caleb.

"He's right," Caleb said with a quirk of his shoulders. "He left a few weeks ago without even picking up his last check."

Cole frowned. Now to the other part. "Mr. Sangston, when and where was your son Caleb born?"

A tired but defeated look settled in the man's weary eyes. He glanced at Caleb, then back at them. "Why do you want to know?"

Joey suddenly shifted. "Do you know Donna or Leland Hendricks?"

He ducked his head, avoided her gaze.

Joey removed a photo from her purse, one of her parents when they were younger. One where she and Justin had both been captured in the shot. "This is a photo of my parents," Joey said. "And that's me when I was thirteen and my little brother when he was two."

Sangston swiped at his wrinkled forehead where sweat beaded in a pool. "I...guess I knew some day it would come to this."

Caleb's eyes narrowed. "What's wrong, Dad?"

A sheen of tears clouded the old man's eyes. "I told you that you were adopted, son, but that's not really true." He took the picture from Joey and handed it to Caleb, who studied it with a quiet intensity that reminded Joey of his mother, not Leland with his hot-headed ways.

"When you were two, someone left you on our doorstep," Sangston said, emotions thick in his voice. "Your mama and I...we'd never been able to have children. We thought you were a miracle God sent to us, and we took you in."

"Mr. Sangston," Cole interjected, "Joey's younger brother, Justin Hendricks, was kidnapped and thought to have been murdered at that time. It was all over the news. Didn't you call the authorities or even consider that this boy you found might have been him?"

Sangston shook his head. "I…don't read," he said in a low voice. "Never learned how. Besides, we were forty miles away from where that happened." His voice rose with conviction. "Then later, when we heard about the kidnapping and possible murder of the Hendricks child, we heard his parents were to blame. Figured the boy was better off with us."

"Where is your wife now?" Cole asked.

"She passed on a few years back. Cancer."

"You mean I might be the Hendricks kid?"

Cole nodded. "It's possible."

Caleb suddenly dropped into a chair with a thud. "Then why didn't those people look for me?" Anger made his voice break as he turned a pained look toward Joey.

"We did." Joey reached out a hand to

cover his. "But all this time, we thought you were dead."

Cole gritted his teeth. Joey thought he had died. But if Donna had been sending money to the ranch, then she might have known he was alive.

What about Leland?

"So you don't know who left the baby?" Cole asked.

Sangston shook his head. "We found him wrapped in a blanket on the porch with a note that asked us to please take care of him, that he needed a loving family."

Joey's gaze jerked to his. "Did you keep the note and blanket?"

"The blanket, yes. Caleb loved it as a child." He hesitated. "I'm afraid my wife threw away the note."

"She didn't want the baby to be found," Cole said matter-of-factly.

The old man gave Caleb an apologetic, sad look, then gripped the table to pull himself up. He had bad knees, Joey realized, and he was aging, but he loved the boy.

The boy—her brother.

Caleb/Justin looked confused, in shock as he stared at the photo, then back to her. They were turning his world upside down.

Joey ached to say more, to hug him and tell him how sorry she was that he'd been stolen from her family's arms. But she had to make certain he really was her brother.

Although she knew in her heart that he was. She glanced at his hand and noticed a birthmark on his wrist, and her throat convulsed. Justin had had a birthmark in that same place.

How would he feel when he learned that his parents might have been involved in his disappearance? That one or both of them conspired to fake a kidnapping/murder for insurance money?

"Here it is." Sangston loped in, carrying a small blue blanket. It was tattered, worn and resurrected a mountain of memories that sent tears to Joey's eyes.

She clutched the blanket in her hands, studying the frayed corner that Justin used to press against his cheek at night. "Oh, my heavens. This is it." Tears trickled down her cheeks. "You used to carry this around all the time. You couldn't sleep without it. You called it your binkie—"

"Binkie," Caleb said at the same time.

Joey smiled and swiped at her eyes. "I can't believe it. All this time I thought about you, felt guilty, prayed you were alive, and now you're here."

Caleb wrestled with his hands, the strain of Sangston's declaration and her appearance evident on his face. "If you're my sister, why did our parents give me away?"

Joey's heart broke. "It's a long story, Justin—"

"My name is Caleb," he said through gritted teeth.

Joey tried not to react to his anger. For God's sake, she understood it. Knew forging a relationship with him would take time. But at least he was alive.

"Maybe we should come back another day," Joey said softly. "Give you and your… father time to talk. Give you time to absorb all this, Caleb."

He sipped his tea, the ice clinking in his glass. "No. I want to know everything. I'm not a kid anymore."

No, he wasn't two. But he was still her baby brother. And all her protective instincts surfaced. "I realize that," she said. "But our family…what happened, it's complicated. Not all pleasant."

A calm anger seemed to radiate over him, reminding her of Donna again.

Joey glanced at Sangston for a cue as to how to proceed. The man was hurting, but he seemed resigned. And he obviously adored Caleb. "He deserves to know about his real family. Then he can decide what to do with the information."

Thankful Justin had had a loving family, she explained about her parents' divorce, their bitter fights, Donna's drinking, Leland's affair then marriage to Lou Anne. Justin listened intently, his hands wiping at the water droplets on his glass as she described the horrible fire that night.

"I searched everywhere for you," Joey said, her voice breaking. "I was so upset. And so were Mom and Rosa. Then Dad heard about the fire and rushed over. He was frantic."

His gaze met hers, and he looked impossibly young again, the same little boy she'd rocked in her arms. "They looked for me?"

"Yes, for months. Donna kept a private investigator on retainer for a long time after that. But the police found blood and they thought you had probably died." She hesitated, then spilled the rest of the sordid story. "After that, the police speculated that Leland, our father, might have orchestrated a fake kidnapping and murder in order to collect on an insurance policy, but there wasn't proof. And when no ransom note came, the police believed that plan had gone awry, or that you had really been kidnapped. But there were never any real leads."

When she finished, he looked torn between anger, shock, bewilderment and confusion. Then affection and fury mingled as he faced Sangston. "I wish you'd told me."

"I didn't know everything. And…your mother and I wanted you to be old enough to handle the truth."

Cole had been quiet, intense while she'd relayed her story. He gestured toward the blanket. "I'd like to take that to the crime lab to be analyzed." He pointed to a small dark stain in the corner. "That looks like a blood-stain. It might be too old to pick up anything, but it's worth a try." He paused, then stroked a finger over his badge absentmindedly. "And we'll need a DNA sample to verify you really are Justin Hendricks."

The boy and Sangston traded looks, then Sangston nodded and Caleb agreed.

Joey pinched her fingers together to keep from pulling Justin's hand in hers and comforting him the way she had when he was two. She knew the DNA would prove he was her brother. Donna's child.

But she didn't think Leland was the father. The more she'd studied him, she recognized subtle nuances of another man's face. A man she knew all too well. A man who had been in Justice the time of the alleged kidnapping and murder. A man who'd helped try to pin the case on her father and Jim McKinney. A man who'd known Lou Anne.

A man who must have also had an affair with Donna…

COLE STUDIED the boy and man, grateful for the rancher's cooperation. He should have reported the baby's sudden appearance on his doorstep years ago and had impeded the investigation, but on some subtle level, Cole sensed Justin—Caleb—had been just as well off growing up on the ranch.

But he had been denied the truth.

And Joey had been denied her brother, and suffered guilt from losing him that night.

He cradled her hand in his, recognizing the strength it took for her not to wrap the boy in her embrace. Joey was an amazing woman. A survivor.

They had to interview Donna again. And Leland. He'd force the truth from them this time. Joey and Justin both deserved answers.

"We should go now." He stood, carefully assessing the situation. He didn't think the old man would run but he wasn't certain. "Mr. Sangston, if the DNA proves Caleb is Justin Hendricks, you'll have to come in and make a formal statement."

"Will he face charges?" Caleb asked, jumping to his defense. "Please say he won't, Sergeant McKinney. I mean if my parents planned a fake kidnapping and murder, they didn't deserve to keep me."

Joey's expression looked tortured. "Nothing was ever proven," she clarified. "I know they've grieved for you, Justin. I mean Caleb. Just like I have."

His young face fell. "I don't want to lose my dad here or for him to get in trouble."

Joey pressed a hand to his shoulder. "Don't worry, Caleb. I work for the governor. You were innocent in all this, and I'll see that the man who loved and raised you isn't charged."

Cole shot her a warning look. She couldn't make that promise. Then again, he didn't know for sure how much power she had over Governor Grange.

"I'd like to see you again," Joey said softly. "When you're ready, Caleb, I'll be here." She removed a business card from her purse and dropped it on the table, then gave Sangston a genuine smile. "I won't intrude on your family, but if Caleb is my brother as I suspect, I'd like some kind of relationship with him. No pressure, though."

Sangston scrubbed a hand over his craggy face. "Thank you, Miss Hendricks. My wife and I...we loved Caleb like he was our own. I'd do anything for him."

Tears dampened Joey's eyes, but she blinked them away, then leaned over and gave the old man a hug. "Thank you for keeping him safe and loving him all these years. I...owe you for that."

Caleb stood and moved to Sangston's side, but gave Joey a tentative smile.

"One more question," Cole said. "Mr. Sangston, did you receive a monthly check for Caleb? A thousand dollars?"

Sangston's chin quivered as he nodded.

"It came from Donna Hendricks?" Joey asked bluntly.

"I did get a check, but it came through St. Francis church. I...honestly had no idea who donated the money. The church said it was from a Good Samaritan."

Cole shifted and tucked his thumbs in his belt loops but refrained from commenting. "We'll call you when we receive the DNA results."

He nodded, and Joey gave Caleb a last longing look, then walked outside into the hot air. By the time they reached the car, and she'd situated herself inside, her shoulders were shaking and tears rolled down her cheeks.

Cole started the car, flipped on the air conditioner, then drove down the long winding driveway from the ranch to the main road. Damn. He tried to harden himself to her emotions. Had to confront her parents. Maybe arrest them.

And he wasn't supposed to care.

But hell. He'd always been a sucker for a woman in trouble. Especially long-legged blondes with eyes that haunted him. And a heart that was just as beautiful.

Ignoring the fact that Zane had warned him not to trust her, he hauled the car to the side of the road beneath a cluster of sprawling trees, then cradled her in his arms and held her.

If Donna had been sending money to the ranch, she had to have known about the boy. He wanted to strangle her for not telling Joey.

"I CAN'T BELIEVE IT, Cole," Joey cried. "I can't believe he's really alive." She hated the onslaught of emotions, but she couldn't control them. It had taken all her restraint not to break down in front of Justin.

"I know it's a shock." Cole stroked her back, his voice soothing but troubled.

She let the tears fall until she felt spent and exhausted. But slowly as her shock wore off and she began to calm, the full implications of their visit registered. A sick feeling stole into her stomach as she put the pieces together. Finally she pushed back, dried her eyes and looked up at Cole.

"Oh, my heavens, Cole. You think Donna knows that Justin is alive?"

A muscle ticked in his broad jaw. "It's possible."

Anger and betrayal knifed through her as the realization kicked in. "She sent money to that ranch every month. She had to have been sending it to him."

Cole tucked a damp strand of her hair behind her ear. "Shh, don't jump to conclusions. There may be another possibility."

Rage built inside her. How could Donna have allowed her to believe her brother was dead all these years if she'd known the truth? And Leland? If he didn't know, keeping the truth from him was cruel as well. "What other explanation could there be?"

Cole shrugged. "Perhaps a nun at the church where Donna sends the money told her about a charity that supports abandoned kids. Maybe Donna thought she was helping an orphan, not necessarily Justin."

Joey considered the idea. Knew it was a long shot. But she latched onto it.

"I have to know," she said quietly. "I'm going to call Donna and Leland. Have them both meet us at the lab where we're taking the blanket."

It was a dicey move. But their options were running out. The blanket might just be the straw that would break the camel's back and send all Donna and Leland's secrets spilling over.

"You call Donna. I'll phone Leland."

She nodded and punched in her mother's number, while Cole stepped from the car to phone Leland. Donna's voice wavered at Joey's request.

"What is this about, Joey?"

"Just meet me there, Mother. It's important." She hung up without giving her mother time to respond, then punched in another number. She had to talk to the governor. Find out how much he knew. If he had slept with Lou Anne. If he and Donna had had an affair. If Justin might be his…

And if he'd known…

If he had, would he have hunted for him? Or would he have wanted Donna to keep the child's paternity a secret? What if Lou Anne had discovered the truth and had met with him to blackmail him?

Then he, too, had a motive for murder.

Chapter Thirteen

Cole and Joey had a late lunch on the way to the crime lab in Dallas, taking time to discuss their strategy. Cole's thoughts were troubled as Joey sat stonily beside him, staring out the window, her eyes still red rimmed from her crying jag. She chewed on her bottom lip and curled her arms around her waist as if struggling to hold on to her last thread of hope that her parents hadn't deceived her.

On the other hand, he also sympathized with the young boy. How would Caleb/Justin handle learning his father had planned a fake kidnapping/ murder for money? What kind of price did a man put on his child's safety?

Leland hadn't been much of a father to

Joey, either. He'd been too focused on his financial problems, on his bitterness toward his first wife and keeping secrets to love his daughter.

Seemed neither the McKinneys nor Hendrickses knew much about raising a family.

Another reason he never intended to get tied down with anyone. He liked women, but he'd never been able to commit, just like his old man. He'd probably make a sorry excuse for a father.

His hands tightened around the steering wheel. Why the hell was he thinking about fatherhood? The subject had never entered his brain before.

Caleb—Justin. Joey. That was the problem.

Joey was getting beneath his skin and making him care about her.

Traffic thickened as he approached the Dallas lab. If the blood on the blanket was Justin's, they'd know they had the right kid. And if there was a second type…maybe they'd learn who had abducted the toddler.

Joey's breathing sounded unsteady as he parked at the lab, and they stepped onto the asphalt. The heat felt oppressive, the noisy traffic sounds deafening. He much preferred the ranches, farmland, woods and open-air spaces.

The freedom.

Yet as they entered the building and the elevator, the urge to comfort Joey was so strong he drew her to him. "Joey, are you all right?"

A flash of pain and worry darkened her expression, but resolve and strength emanated from her. "I have to know the truth. It's past time."

He admired her courage as they went inside. He identified himself as Sergeant Cole McKinney, and they were shown to the lead investigator's, Simmons's, office, the same detective Cole had consulted about the ballistics test.

Cole explained about the blanket, and Simmons secured it in an evidence bag. "I'll get someone on it ASAP."

An hour later, the receptionist appeared at the door to inform them that Donna had arrived. Donna rushed into the front office, her hair perfectly coiffed, her dress a white linen that made her look cool and composed in spite of the soaring temperatures and stressful situation.

"What's this about, Joey?"

"Sit down, Mother. I want to wait until Leland arrives before we proceed."

The first sign of panic lined Donna's mouth as she chewed on her lip. "Joey, I don't know what's going on, but think long and hard about what you're going to say and do today."

"I have, Mother," Joey said through clenched teeth. "Now sit down."

Donna spotted the baby blanket in the plastic bag, and the color drained from her face. She slumped into the chair, twining her fingers together. The silence roared with tension as they waited for Leland, but finally he arrived, his face ruddy from rushing in the heat.

Annoyance and anger colored his eyes as he seated himself in the chair adjacent to Donna.

"Mr. and Mrs. Hendricks," Cole began. "We've asked you here because we may have some new evidence concerning the disappearance of your son, Justin."

Donna's gaze shot back to the baby blanket, and Leland's mouth gaped.

Cole picked up the bagged blanket and held it in front of him. "Do either of you recognize this?"

Donna's lower lip quivered. "Yes, that belonged to my baby. He always slept with it."

Detective Simmons accepted it from Cole. "I'll take it for testing now."

Cole nodded. "Did you see that blanket after Justin was kidnapped?"

Donna shook her head and twined her manicured fingers in her lap again. "No, it was missing. I...whoever took Justin must have taken it with him."

"Where the hell did you find it?" Leland asked.

Joey cleared her throat. "Donna has been sending money to a church every month. For $1,000, to be exact. The nun there sends the money on to a ranch."

Leland stood, his tone rising, "What does that have to do with Justin's baby blanket?"

Cole threw up a warning hand. "Sit down, Leland. We'll get to that."

Leland's look of fury was so hot it could have melted butter, but he knotted his hands into fists and reclaimed the seat.

"We just visited that ranch," Joey said. Underneath her calm tone, Cole sensed the barely suppressed rage and hurt. "And guess what we found, Mother?"

Donna gripped the armrest, then glanced away from Joey. Outside a storm cloud passed, covering the sun, and casting gray shadows across the room.

"Mother, it's time to come clean." Joey gripped the edges of the armrest and shoved her face into her mother's, forcing Donna's gaze back to her. "I saw him."

"I don't know what you're talking about," Donna declared.

"Stop lying. Don't you get it, it's over!" Joey's breath hissed with anger. "I saw him. We have his baby blanket. We're going to test the DNA." She shook the chair, rattling Donna. "Now tell me the truth. You sent money to that ranch because the boy who lives there, the one named Caleb, who was adopted by a couple named the Sangstons, is Justin, isn't he?"

Leland flattened his hand against his heart and made a choking sound in his throat. Donna's hand flew to her mouth but Joey refused to feel sorry for her.

"Tell me, Mother. I have a right to the truth." She gestured toward her father. "Even Leland deserves to know if Justin is alive!"

"Yes," Donna screeched, her calm disintegrating. "Yes, Justin is alive. I c...an't believe you found him."

Joey's heart ached. "How could you have done this, Mother?" She glanced once more at her father, wanting to hate him, too, but the stunned look on his face indicated that he had no knowledge of Justin's whereabouts.

Donna reached for her, but Joey backed away, shaking her head violently.

"How could you have lied to me all these years? Made me believe Justin was dead? You let me blame myself for his disappearance." Joey choked on the last sentence, the anguish from her childhood resurfacing.

"Just listen, Joey—" Donna began.

"Listen to what? Excuses?" Joey wanted

to shake her, to make her suffer as she had. "What did you do? Plan the fake kidnapping and murder to keep him away from Dad, then whisk Justin away to that ranch?" Her voice grew colder. "Did you pay someone to cover for you?"

"It's not like that," Donna said. "I did not plan that kidnapping." Donna aimed a suspicious look at Leland. "I'm guessing your father did that. He wanted the insurance money and he wanted to hurt me."

Leland slammed his fist against the desk, jarring papers. "How dare you accuse me of foul play when you've been caught lying?"

Donna jumped up, waving her arms, her calm disintegrating. "I didn't plan the kidnapping. You did, Leland, to hurt me. You had someone steal my son during that fire, didn't you?" She whirled on Joey. "I was devastated, you know that, Joey. I thought Justin was dead for a long time. You have to believe me."

Joey steeled herself against Donna, not trusting anything her parents uttered.

"But I never gave up looking for him. Even after Leland did, I kept searching. I hired a private investigator with my own money." She pressed a hand over her heart. "I just couldn't let myself believe that my baby boy was really dead. I felt in here, that he was still alive. Out there somewhere." Her voice broke. "At night, I used to wake up and hear him crying for me. Saying Mama. I wanted to die inside, too."

"When did you find him?" Cole asked.

Donna clasped her hands together. "About ten years ago. The P.I. got a lead. He called me and I went to this church in Dallas and saw this little boy there. He was with a man and a woman, a family called the Sangstons. They owned a ranch near Mineral Wells." She inhaled and rushed on. "The minute I laid eyes on that boy, I knew he was my son, Justin. I wanted to tear him away from them."

"Why didn't you come forward then?" Cole asked.

"Because Leland still had custody and you knew you'd lose him again," Joey interjected.

Donna twisted to glare at her, then Leland. "That was part of it. But Justin looked happy with those people, and I could tell they loved him, and I realized that if I spoke out, it would rock his world upside down. For once, I tried not to be selfish."

Joey cut her a scathing look, but Donna continued, "By then, you hated me, Joey, and Leland...he never cared about Justin. He didn't deserve to know he was alive, much less to have custody of him again."

"And why didn't he care?" Joey said, venom lacing her voice. "I always wondered why it was so easy for Dad to have used his own son in a devious plan to extract money."

Donna's eyes went wild. "Joey..."

"Justin wasn't Leland's son, was he, Mother?"

"Be quiet, Joey," Donna sputtered. "You don't know what you're saying."

"Don't I, Mother?" Joey stared at her mother in disgust. "You blamed Leland for his infidelity and were so bitter, that you had an affair of your own."

"Joey, stop it!" Donna ordered.

Leland collapsed back into the seat and scrubbed his hand over his face, sweating.

"What I don't understand is that if you'd

confessed that Daddy wasn't Justin's father, you probably could have won custody of Justin."

"That's not true," Donna said, her voice trembling. "With my drinking problem, no judge was going to give me custody. Justin would have been put in foster care. That would have been awful."

"Or maybe his real father would have raised him," Joey shot back. "Or did his real father even know about him? Did you keep that as another one of your tawdry secrets?"

COLE KEPT HIS SPINE straight as he watched Joey grappling with her feelings. She seemed to be holding her breath while she waited for her mother's answer, but Donna clammed up and refused to talk further. Leland stood and moved toward the door, his expression lethal as he whipped his head toward Donna, then Joey.

"I have to get out of here," he said in a harsh voice. "I'll talk to you later, Joey."

She simply stared at him, a wealth of turmoil in the silence that stretched between them.

"Don't leave town, Mr. Hendricks," Cole

said. "We may want to question you again when we get the results of these DNA tests."

Leland gave him an icy stare, then walked out the door and slammed it behind him.

Donna stood and smoothed down her linen suit, touched her hair as if to tuck it back in place, along with her lies. "I want you to think long and hard about how you handle this information," she said to Joey. "I've kept up with your brother over the years, and he's happy."

"I know, I saw him," Joey said.

Donna swayed slightly. "You told him?"

"His adopted father and I did, yes."

"My God." Donna pressed a trembling hand to her cheek. "How did he take it? Do you think he'll want to see us?"

The hope that flickered in Donna's eyes surprised Cole. Maybe Donna really did love the boy and wanted what was best for him.

"I don't know, Mother." Joey wheezed a tired breath. "He's going to need time to process everything."

"I wouldn't contact him yet," Cole warned. "After all, the investigation is not over."

Donna's eyes turned into glaciers as she frowned at Cole. "Hasn't our family suffered enough already?"

Cole towered over her. "What about Lou Anne Wallace and her daughter, Sarah? They suffered. Someone has to pay for their deaths, Mrs. Hendricks."

"I didn't kill them." Donna gave Joey a beseeching look. "Please, Joey. For your brother's sake, handle this with discretion."

"I took care of Justin when he was little and you were drunk, Mother," Joey said bitterly. "I'll do everything I can to protect him now. Even if it means protecting him from you and Daddy."

JOEY COLLAPSED into the chair, drained as Donna left the room, leaving a cloud of suspicion in her wake.

"Joey?"

Cole's deep voice barely penetrated the fog surrounding her.

He knelt beside her and cradled her hands in his, warming them with his own. "Joey, do you know who Justin's real father is?"

The million-dollar question. She had a good idea. But could she implicate the governor of Texas without talking to him first? Without proof?

Dread swelled in her chest. She hated to lie to Cole. Still, she couldn't be certain yet. "I…I'm not sure."

Cole's blue eyes blazed a path over her face. "Then how did you know that Leland wasn't his father?"

Joey shrugged, vying for calm. "I didn't. I just played a hunch." She searched Cole's face, praying he'd understand. "When I saw Caleb, Justin, I thought he looked like Donna. The way he rode with such confidence was just like her."

He nodded.

"But then I searched his face for signs of Leland, and I…didn't see any of our father in him." She struggled to recall conversations she'd overheard when she was a teenager. Before Justin was born and afterward. "It always bothered me that Dad could have used his own son for money. Then I remembered my parents fighting. Leland calling him 'your' son." She squeezed Cole's hands, clutched them to her, absorbing his strength. Oddly his presence calmed her, gave her a sense of balance amidst the storm of feelings raging inside her. "Now it makes sense."

"If Leland knew Justin wasn't his, why did he fight for custody?" Cole asked.

"To get back at Donna," Joey said, her mind spinning. "And if Lou Anne suspected or found out Justin wasn't my father's, that would have been another reason she balked against raising him."

"You're right." Cole stroked the palm of her hand. "But if she'd threatened to tell, Donna might have wanted to shut her up. Leland probably wouldn't have been happy about it, either."

Another reason he might have killed Lou Anne. To save face.

"So might the real father," Joey said, her heart in her throat.

The door screeched open, and Detective Simmons poked his head in. "Is it safe now?"

Cole mumbled a yes, and Simmons strode in. "I spoke with our lab techs. They examined the bloodstain and are pretty sure it's too old to pick up anything, but they'll give it a try."

Joey sighed in frustration, then an idea struck her. "We don't have to disclose that information. Why don't we leak that we know who the DNA belongs to and see if we can smoke out the killer?"

Her heart raced although other complications made her rethink the plan. Going public meant that Justin/Caleb would find out the truth. Then again, he was old enough to deal with it, she hoped. She only prayed he'd forgive her part in exposing it.

"Joey?" Cole's deep, throaty voice washed over her. "It's a good plan. But are you having doubts?"

Oh, yeah. But she had to do what was right. "No. I know just who to call. Harold Dennison."

Cole nodded. "And I'll call Zane, Sloan, Anna and Sheriff Matheson and tell them to meet us at the courthouse in Justice. I want everyone there when the news hits town."

He punched in Zane's number, and when he finished, Joey borrowed his phone. She'd left hers at the inn. Harold Dennison seemed stunned by her call, but she promised him an exclusive when the story broke, and he agreed to run the story that afternoon.

A mixture of excited anticipation and dread pitted Joey's stomach as she disconnected the call, and she and Cole walked to the car. By nightfall, they might have the answers to the puzzle that had gone unsolved for fifteen years. Maybe Lou Anne and Sarah Wallace's killer would be behind bars.

But which one of their suspects would it be: Jim McKinney? Her father? Her mother?

Or the man she was almost certain was Justin's father, Governor Grange?

ADRENALINE RACED through Cole as he drove back toward Justice. Zane had agreed to have all the suspects meet at the courthouse. In light of this new revelation and the leaking of information to the press, they were bound to push one of them into a confession. Although Donna and Leland hadn't broken yet…

And what about Jim? Or Stella?

His stomach knotted as a sickening

thought occurred to him. If Leland wasn't Justin's father, and Donna had had an affair, whom had she slept with? Leland had been with Lou Anne and Lou Anne had slept with Jim McKinney. Dear God, what if his father had slept with Donna?

Nausea bolted through him. The connection still wouldn't make him related to Joey, but it would mean that Justin might be his half brother.

He scrubbed a hand over his face, deciding not to alarm Joey with his speculations. He would talk to Jim McKinney, though. Find out if he'd slept with Donna.

The scenario played through his head. Years ago, both Donna and Jim had a drinking problem. Jim claimed he didn't know what had happened the night Lou Anne died. What if she discovered that her lover was also sleeping with Leland's ex-wife? That the child Leland wanted her to raise was Jim McKinney's?

He cut his gaze toward Joey, but she'd closed her eyes and rested her head against the back of the seat. Night was falling and shadows streaked her pale face. He didn't have the heart to trouble her with more theories, especially unfounded ones.

The traffic and noise of the city gave way to countryside, and the road was nearly deserted. He checked the rearview mirror and saw bright lights approaching. Déjà vu from the earlier hit-and-run sent a ripple of anxiety along his nerve endings. Ahead, a tractor-trailer raced toward him. He flashed his lights, signaling for the driver to switch to low beams, but he weaved across the centerline as if he'd fallen asleep.

A pickup truck pulled out from a side road, too, a little too slowly, and crawled across the road in front of him. He swerved to avoid it and the truck, and saw the river approaching. Suddenly the car behind him slammed into him, and sent him into a spin.

Joey's eyes jerked open. "God, not again."

"I'm afraid so." He hit the gas hoping to outrun it, but the car crashed into him again with a vicious thud, and he lost control. The sedan spun a hundred and eighty degrees, then skidded and raced toward the embankment. Tires ground and churned on the asphalt. Metal screeched and splintered.

Joey screamed, and water rushed up to meet them as the car nose-dived into the edge of the river and plunged toward the murky bottom.

Chapter Fourteen

Joey braced herself for the impact of the accident, used her hands to block the force of the air bag, then immediately reached for the seat belt. This time, thank God, the belt slid free.

"Joey?"

"I'm all right. You?"

"Yeah." He released a string of expletives, then tore at her air bag again. "We're sinking. Got to get out."

She tried her door but it refused to budge. "My door is stuck."

He was pushing on his. "Hold your breath. Water will rush in when I open the door."

She inhaled a sharp breath, then did as he instructed while he used his shoulder to shove against the weight. The current swept them up, carrying the car deeper and further into the river. Seconds later, icy water flowed into the car, rising quickly to her neck as he opened the door. Cole reached for her hand, and she latched onto his, grateful for the contact as he yanked her out of the sinking car and through the murky water. A chill slithered up her spine as they battled the current. She kicked and fought, determined to survive. Her knee hit a jagged rock and pain sliced along her leg. She clawed for the surface, propelling her arms forward as the water dragged her and Cole apart. Gasping for air, she broke the surface, but the current trapped her and sucked her back under.

"Joey!"

She struggled under the surface, swimming toward Cole, then finally pushed upward enough to lift her head above the water. He swam toward her, but the current tried to drag her the other way. She was losing steam. Her legs ached, her arms throbbed, her lungs begged for air.

Then suddenly Cole grabbed her around the waist and dragged her upward. She kicked, moving on autopilot, furious that someone had almost killed them when they were so close to solving the case.

The call…Dennison. He had already leaked the news and the killer knew they were closing in. He might be here now. Waiting for them. Watching them, hoping they'd drown.

Determination mushroomed inside her chest, and her strength rallied long enough for her to break the surface again, then she gasped in a breath and began to swim alongside Cole. It seemed like miles as they fought the water and made their way toward a tree overhanging the deepest part of the river. A branch had splintered in a recent storm, and Cole grabbed it and used it to haul himself forward. He thrust out his hand, and she grabbed it and kicked while he pulled her to the branch. She clutched it with shaky fingers and maneuvered her body along the thick length until they crawled onto the embankment.

Joey's arms felt ragged as she collapsed onto the grassy edge. Then they glanced up in horror to see a rifle pointed at them.

Heavens, no. They'd survived the crash only to have the killer waiting.

She blinked away the water and murk, shoving at her tangled hair, then lost her breath when she saw the person holding the gun.

Not Donna or Leland. Or Jim McKinney. Not even Governor Grange.

The one person she'd trusted unconditionally—Rosa.

COLE HEAVED for air, silently thanking God he had managed to get himself and Joey to safety. But the sight of the rifle barrel and the frantic-looking woman holding it froze the blood in his veins. Her eyes looked wild and panicked, and her arm was trembling so badly he feared she'd accidentally press the trigger.

"You wouldn't leave things alone," Rosa wailed. "I begged you, Miss Joey. I begged you to think of your mama."

"Rosa, put the gun down," Cole said, using a tone meant to calm her but one that reeked of authority.

"You don't want to hurt us, Rosa," Joey rasped. "You know you don't." Joey lifted her hand, but Rosa stabbed at her with the blunt end of the gun.

"Don't move, or I'll shoot you both."

Cole gestured for Joey to drop her hand, and she did, but shock tightened her features.

"You helped raise me, Rosa," Joey whispered. "Justin and I both loved you. You were part of our family. Special to us." She hesitated, cleared her throat. "If you're doing this to protect my mother, it's not worth it. I've already talked to her. I know Justin is alive. I saw him with my own eyes."

Rosa made a strangled sound. "You were never supposed to find him. Never supposed to know. You were free to go on with your own life."

"Go on with my life?" Joey's voice vibrated with pain. "How could I do that when I blamed myself for his death?"

Rosa pushed at the loose strands of her black braid. She looked tired and at her wits' end. "Justin was safe and happy with the Sangstons. Now you mess everythin' up."

"I'm glad he was happy," Joey said in a strained voice. "But he's my family. I had a right to know where he was."

"Family…I did everything for family, to

protect little Justin." Rosa's voice broke. "Family is all that matters."

Joey knotted a fist over her heart. "But I was your family, too."

"You don't understand. You were older, Joey. Strong. I knew you would be okay no matter what." Rosa's English became garbled with a few words of Spanish. "Justin, my little boy, Mr. Leland…he was going to have him kidnapped. I had to stop it."

"So you took him?" Cole interjected. "Before Leland could put his plan into effect?"

Rosa nodded, tears tracking down her cheeks. "He didn't love Justin. Knew he wasn't his bebé. He hated Donna for pretending like he was. He was d…esperate for the money."

"So you heard about his plan and you set the fire that night?" Cole asked.

"The fire! Oh, my goodness. You set it!" Joey staggered. "Rosa, we could have been killed."

"No, no…" Rosa wailed. "I called firemen, get us out. No danger, not really." Her crazed expression alarmed Cole. "My cousin, he got the bebé. Took him to the ranch. I know the family. My cousin, Hector, he work their ranch. The Sangstons, they want bebé of their own. They good people. Love our Justin." Rosa's voice grew colder. "Not like Ms. Donna back then, drinking. Or Mr. Leland. Always think of themselves. Pass bebé back and forth like he sack of flour."

"But my mother found out where Justin was," Joey said, obviously trying to make sense of it all. "Did you tell her, or did she find him on her own?"

"I not tell her." Rosa gulped, the gun wavering. "Not at first. But my cousin—"

"Hector Elvarez," Cole supplied.

Rosa nodded. "He tell me Ms. Donna hire man to hunt for Justin. Then Ms. Donna, she change. She not drinking by then. She make right choice. Leave little Justin be. Best thing for everyone."

"Except I didn't know, Rosa," Joey cried.

"What about Lou Anne Wallace?" Cole asked. "She found out about Leland's plan and called Donna, didn't she?"

"She a mess, too. Mean to our Justin."

Rosa's voice shook with agitation. "She going to tell everyone Justin not Mr. Leland's. I have to stop her or little Justin be take away. Foster care. Strangers. Not ever see him again."

Cole tried to inject calmness into his voice. "And you killed Sarah Wallace when she came to town because she found out what you'd done?"

Rosa broke into a sob. "Not want to, but my sister, she sick now, needs Rosa to take care of her. Couldn't go to jail or let Justin be found."

"You tried to strangle Anna, too?" Joey asked in horror. Rosa nodded, tears filling her eyes.

"What about Sheriff Mattheson and the fire at the jail? Did you set that?" Cole asked.

Rosa shook her head. "Hector, but he only wanted to protect me."

"Where is he now?" Cole asked. "Back in Mexico?"

Rosa nodded. Her eyes pleaded with Joey to understand. "I check on Justin, Miss Joey.

I see him every Sunday, at church. He growin' up. Big strong man, good rider."

"I know," Joey said, her tone more even now. "I saw him, and he is happy. He loves his new family." She started to rise, and Cole reached to stop her, but she gently pulled away from him. "The Sangstons were good to him, much better than Donna and Leland would have been."

"The mama, Mrs. Sangston, before she go, she tell me how much her son mean to her."

"Did she know that Donna had found him?" Joey asked.

"She guessed. I tell her Ms. Donna different. Only want her boy happy."

"That's right, Rosa. And you did what you did for our family." Joey inched closer, but Rosa thrust the gun up, and Cole's breath lodged in his throat.

"Rosa, you can't hurt me, I know you can't. Justin has met me now. You don't want him to think that you killed his sister."

Rosa's hand sagged, and she sobbed louder. "I so sorry...so sorry, Miss Joey—"

Joey grabbed Rosa, and they wrestled with

the gun. It went off, but the shot pinged into a tree. Cole pushed Joey aside, and pried the weapon from Rosa's hands. She collapsed onto the ground in a fit of tears.

Cole clutched the gun and reached inside his pocket for his phone. But water had ruined it. Damn.

He glanced at Joey, wondering if he should tie Rosa to restrain her, but Joey slumped down by Rosa and cradled her in her arms.

Rosa leaned into her, crying. "I'm so sorry, Joey, so sorry."

"I'm going to flag someone down and call for help," Cole said.

Rosa removed a cell phone from her skirt pocket and slipped it into Joey's hands. Joey handed it to Cole, and Cole stepped away to call Zane and Sloan.

A DEEP SADNESS pervaded Joey as Zane McKinney snapped handcuffs around Rosa's wrists. Rosa had loved her brother and her more than Donna and Leland had, yet in her panicked attempt to help them, she'd still hurt them.

And she'd taken two lives during the process and almost taken others.

Did Donna know about Rosa's guilt? Had she covered for her all this time?

"We still have to question Donna," Cole said as if he'd read her mind. "See if she conspired to keep the truth from the police."

"And my father has to answer for the fake kidnapping/murder plan."

Her body throbbed and ached with fatigue, though. "Could we do that tomorrow? I... don't think I can handle anything more tonight."

Cole pulled her up against him. "I think that can be arranged. It'll take a while for Zane and Sloan to process Rosa. I'll tell them to make some calls, and we can set up the interrogation for the morning."

"By then news of Rosa's arrest will have hit the papers," Joey said sadly.

Cole squeezed her hand, then went to speak to his half brothers. She wiped at tears as they situated Rosa into a squad car. Sloan handed Cole his car keys, and he rode with Zane, while Cole drove her back to the inn. She expected Donna to confront them, but thankfully she must not have received word of Rosa's arrest yet. Joey hoped they could forestall it until morning when she'd had time to absorb the shock herself.

Still damp from the river, she shivered as she entered her room. Cole rubbed his hands up and down her arms. "You're soaked and trembling. Why don't you relax in a hot bath, and I'll grab us something to eat."

She ran a hand over his damp clothing. "You're wet, too, Cole. You need to change."

"I'll grab a shower in my room and meet you back here with some food."

Too weary to argue, she nodded and moved into the bathroom. She found a small bottle of bubble bath on the counter, sprinkled some into the tub, then filled it with water. The day's and night's events replayed in her mind like a movie trailer, and she shuddered. How could her family have gotten so messed up? What would Justin—Caleb—do now? Would he want to see her? And what would happen to Donna and Leland?

In the morning, they'd find out. Then she'd talk to Governor Grange.

Or maybe she should get it over with tonight. She retrieved her cell phone and punched in his number, but received his service again. She left a message that it was urgent, that an arrest had been made in the Wallace murders and that she needed to speak to him privately. Then she hung up, contemplating how to handle the situation as she lowered herself into the sea of bubbles and closed her eyes. Slowly she let the heat melt away the soreness and chill in her limbs. But the ache in her heart couldn't be assuaged so easily.

If Governor Grange was Justin's father, did he want to know? Would he want to meet Justin and have a relationship with him? And what would acknowledging an illegitimate son do to his reputation?

How would that revelation affect Justin/Caleb?

Cole. He understood about being an illegitimate child. But he had overcome the stigma and become an honorable man. A formidable Texas Ranger. He was strong, ethical. Smart. Sexy as hell.

And he had saved her life.

She wanted him tonight.

The hotel room door opened, and his deep voice called her name.

"Joey?"

"I'll be out in a minute." She dried off, drained the water from the tub and donned her pale blue cotton robe. When she'd belted it and towel-dried her hair, she stepped into the room. Cole had showered quickly and shaved. His damp hair clung to the ends of his button-down shirt. On the desk, she spotted two cups of steaming soup he must have bought from the bar.

"It's not much," he said, "but I didn't want to go to Donna's and have to explain about Rosa."

"No, I'm not ready to deal with my mother yet, either."

The two of them ate the simple meal in silence. Joey barely tasted the food, but at least the hot soup and bath soothed her nerves. When she looked up at Cole, he was watching her with an intense look in his eyes as if he expected her to fall apart any minute.

"Thank you, Cole."

"Do you feel better?"

His gruff voice skated over raw nerve endings, reminding her of their close brush with death earlier.

"Yes." But she hurt deep inside and didn't think the pain would ease. "I still can't believe that Rosa killed Lou Anne and Sarah Wallace."

"Shh." He stood, set their dishes aside, then threaded his fingers through her hair and hugged her to him. "Don't think about it tonight, sugar."

She lifted her face, and her heart fluttered at the raw need and desire flaming in his eyes.

"I thought we were going to die tonight," she whispered.

He traced his fingers along her arm, and she quivered with longing.

"No one is ever going to hurt you again," he growled. "I promise you, Joey."

"Cole—"

"Shh." The smoldering look he gave her teased at her senses, made her want to believe that she could trust him. That he would be the one man who would never lie to her. Never hurt her.

That he would always be there for her. Take care of her. Love her.

Love?

Heavens, yes. She wanted his loving tonight. The physical touches. The closeness. Even if he didn't say the words or feel them.

THE IMAGE OF JOEY fighting through the water, nearly drowning, then facing Rosa with that gun haunted Cole. He had dealt with life-and-death situations all his life, had put himself on the firing line in the military, had witnessed good men die and taken lives, but not once during those times, had such bone-jarring fear for another person seized him.

He had been terrified of losing Joey.

He didn't like the realization, but he couldn't deny it. Just as he couldn't deny himself the pleasure of taking her to bed now and making her come apart in his arms.

She lay a hand along his neck, teasing him with her fingers, and rational thought fled as a fierce hunger erupted inside him. He had to have her now.

She met his gaze, and raw need flashed in her expression. With a low groan, he cupped her face in his hands. The sweet scent of bubble bath and shampoo invaded his senses as he lowered his head and claimed her mouth with his. She tasted like sultry Texas nights, fiery hot and filled with passion. Enflamed, he deepened the kiss, teasing her lips apart with his tongue and delving inside to play a mating dance with hers.

His hands drifted of their own accord, tracing a path down her shoulders. Then he stripped the flimsy cotton robe from her voluptuous body until she stood naked before him. He drank in the sight of her heavy, bare breasts, nipples rosy and distended; her smooth, flat stomach; and the blond curls waiting for his exploration.

She made a small throaty sound, then pushed at his shirt. He tore it off and threw it on the bed, then claimed her mouth again while his hands covered her breasts, stroking, kneading, twirling the peaks with his thumbs.

"Cole…" she whispered his name against his chest as she lowered her head and spread kisses along his jaw, sucking on his neck and below his ear, then moving her hands down to his belt buckle. Seconds later, she removed it, tossed it to the floor, then his zipper rasped in the darkness. His sex surged hard and aching for her, as she shoved his jeans over his thighs.

He kicked them off, but stopped her hand when she began to stroke him. Instead he lowered her to the bed, climbed above her and suckled her breasts, first one, then the other as his fingers sank deep inside her. She writhed against the sheets, threaded her fingers through his hair, ground her hips up to meet his hand, cried out his name and drove him crazy with her needy sounds of lust.

He licked his way down her belly, planted breathy kisses along the insides of her thighs until his mouth replaced his fingers, and he spread her legs and sank his tongue inside her. She twisted frantically, clawed at his arms and pleaded for more.

"Cole, hmm, that feels so good." She moaned. "I love you…"

Her whispered words made him pause

momentarily—had she only been caught up in the moment?

She traced her finger along the tip of his shaft. "I want you inside me when I come this time...."

Her heady request made his body churn with desire, and he rose above her, shucked off his boxers, grabbed a condom from his pocket and rolled it on. He was panting, perspiration dotting his chest and forehead, his mind clouded with wanting Joey. Joey with her sassy smile, her glorious mane of blond hair and those mile-long legs.

Mile-long legs he'd imagined wrapped around him the first time he'd seen her. Mile-long legs he'd finally get to feel as he rode her.

His length throbbed, hard and pulsing for her heaven, and she reached up, stroked him once, then guided him inside her. The smile of elation and cry of ecstasy when he filled her shattered something inside him. A wall he'd built to keep emotions and sex compartmentalized.

A wall he didn't want to think about now.

He wanted nothing between them but bare skin and hot touches.

She clawed his hips and he thrust deeper, bracing his arms beside her head as he watched her eyes change colors when she finally allowed her release to claim her.

He drove himself harder, faster, deeper, pulled her legs up to hug him, burying himself as far as he could go, then even deeper. She cried his name again, and he thrust inside her again, his body jerking and shaking with the splendor of the moment as heady sensations rocked through him.

Joey trembled from the aftermath of her orgasm, and yet, she wanted Cole again already. She splayed her hands along his chest, toying with the coarse, dark hair grazing his chest, and pressed a kiss to his neck as he rolled sideways, cradling her in his arms.

She wanted to shout her love for him again, and hoped that her declaration hadn't scared him. She couldn't, didn't expect him to return the sentiment. He had come here to do a job and he'd go back to it, and she to hers. She kissed his neck again, and he dropped a kiss into her hair.

"That was amazing."

"Uh-huh." He moaned and cupped her bottom in his hands, dragging her closer so their bodies touched. "I wanted you the first time I laid eyes on those long legs."

She smiled against him. "And I wanted you the moment I saw you haul your big body off that Harley."

He chuckled and trailed his fingers over her breast, causing a thousand titillating sensations to take flight inside her. "When I saw you take that shot of tequila, lick the salt and suck that lime, I wanted your tongue on me."

Joey rubbed his muscled bare calf with her toe. She liked this teasing side of Cole. "And when you closed your mouth on that beer bottle, I imagined your mouth on me."

He lowered his head and kissed her again, long, hard, taking all she offered, asking for more. "I fantasized about your long legs wrapped around my waist."

She trapped his shaft in her hand and stroked, feeling heady as it hardened and pulsed between her fingers. "And I wanted you inside me."

He nuzzled her neck. "Well, sugar, tonight, let's make all your wishes come true."

If only that were true. Because, heaven help her, right now she wished he'd tell her he loved her.

But he did something almost as good. He flipped her to her stomach, crawled on top of her and massaged the knots in her shoulders. His fingers dipped lower to stroke and soothe all her aching places, and soon he thrust inside her again, pumping and grinding, shouting her name, filling her, until she cried out with another soul shattering climax.

Finally she fell asleep, huddled in his embrace, with euphoria still washing over her and his kisses still heating her body.

THE ROOM PHONE JANGLED, jarring Cole from the best damn sleep he'd had in ages. He'd been dreaming about sex and a woman who loved him, a woman who'd never abandon him or cheat on him, a woman who made him want forever.

He shifted, his body flaming again as Joey's curvy backside snuggled deeper against his hard length. His hand snaked out to cup her breasts, and she rewarded him with a soft sigh that only heightened his early morning arousal.

Unfortunately the shrill sound of the phone continued. He cursed, and started to ignore it, but it might be important.

Hell. He really did not want to leave this warm, cozy bed with Joey.

The sound blasted the quiet again, and Joey stirred with a frown. "You'd better get it."

"I know." Reluctantly he dragged his warm hand from her breasts and clicked to answer. "Sergeant Cole McKinney."

"It's Zane. Listen, we've got trouble."

He scrubbed his hands over his face. "What's up?"

"Leland Hendricks has taken Dad hostage."

Cole snapped upright. "What?"

"He's holding him in a cabin in the woods, Cole." Zane's voice reverberated with worry. "You'd better find Joey and tell her. Then meet us at the courthouse ASAP."

The phone clicked into silence with a

deafening thud. Cole glanced down at the beauty in his bed, and grimaced. She'd had a hell of a time the day before.

And this day didn't look like it would be any better.

Chapter Fifteen

Joey leaned on her elbow and braced her head on her hand with a come-back-to-bed expression.

But Cole stiffened, his Texas Ranger face back on as he yanked on his jeans. Disappointment ballooned in her chest, along with the realization that something was wrong.

"Who was that, Cole?"

"Zane." He grabbed his shirt and shrugged it on. "We have to get dressed. Now."

His clipped tone sent her nerves on edge. "What's going on?"

He finally paused, and looked at her, his blue eyes smoky with the remnants of shared memories of the night before, but also filled with turmoil.

A half-dozen scenarios crashed into her

head. Justin had run away or was hurt. Donna was having a fit at the jail wanting Rosa released.

"Cole, you're scaring me."

He hissed a breath, then lowered himself beside her on the bed and cradled her hand in his. "Leland has taken my dad hostage."

Joey gasped. "What?"

"He's holding him at some cabin. Zane wants us to meet him at the courthouse. Then we'll decide what to do."

"But why would my father take Jim as a hostage? What does he want?"

"I don't know yet. But we have to go."

She nodded, numbness creeping over her as the shock settled in. She flew off the bed, adrenaline churning, then ran next door, dug in her suitcase for a clean pair of jeans and shirt and hurriedly dressed. She yanked her hair into a ponytail just as Cole entered. He clipped on his badge and weapon.

Fear clouded her throat. Rosa had been arrested. Her dad was in the clear for murder charges. What in the world was Leland thinking? Did he have a gun on Jim McKinney?

And what would she do if Cole had to shoot her father?

Cole opened the door, and she grabbed her purse. The date book that had belonged to Lou Anne fell out, and Cole frowned. "What's that?"

She snatched it up and stared at it guiltily. She should have told Cole about the book, but she still hadn't spoken to the governor. "Nothing, let's go."

The lie burned her throat as she followed him to the car and climbed in the passenger seat. Her cell phone rang, and she glanced at it, figuring it was an hysterical Donna. But it was the governor instead.

She didn't want to have the conversation in the car, but she had to take the call or Cole would be suspicious. "Joey Hendricks."

"Yes, Joey, it's Governor Grange. I received your message and I'm on my way to Justice. I should be there shortly. Who was arrested for the murders?"

Joey explained about Rosa's part in the murders, as well as Justin's disappearance. "We have another situation now," she told him. "My father has taken Jim McKinney hostage. Sergeant McKinney and I are on the way to meet the other Rangers now and find out what's going on."

"Dear God. It never ends, does it? What the hell is Leland thinking?"

"He must be desperate," Joey said. "Yesterday was rough. He was upset when he left the crime lab. We confronted him with the fact that Justin wasn't his son."

An abrupt silence followed, the tension palpable.

"Governor?"

"I heard you."

Joey waited for a response, but his shaky breathing vibrated over the line. They had reached the courthouse, and Cole climbed out, his brow arched as if asking if she was coming.

"I need to go now," she said. "But we'll talk later."

"Yes," he said in an unusually solemn voice. "I'll see you soon."

Joey hung up, her heart racing as they rushed into the courthouse. Thankfully Harold Dennison hadn't heard a word yet and was nowhere to be seen. But Donna was sitting in the office in a hard wooden chair, her eyes glazed.

"I can't believe you all arrested Rosa." She gave Joey a condemning look. "Rosa loved your little brother. I don't condone her actions, but she did what she did out of love."

Joey's throat clogged with emotions. Her mother didn't have to sound so righteous. Rosa wouldn't have had to take such drastic action if Donna hadn't been an alcoholic and Leland so vindictive and selfish.

"Mother, do you know why Leland has taken Jim McKinney hostage?" Joey asked.

COLE KNOTTED his fists by his sides as Donna turned away, and set her lips into a thin line.

He had a sneaking suspicion that Leland had been pushed to the limit the day before, humiliated by the public revelation that Justin was not his, and he might have jumped to the same conclusion that Cole had.

That Jim McKinney was the boy's father. That he'd slept with Donna, given her a son and had then slept with his new wife as well.

Every man had his breaking point, and Cole could almost understand Leland's twisted need for revenge. If another man touched Joey, he'd want to kill him.

Zane approached him, looking in control although the rigid set to his jaw indicated he had his own concerns. Sloan raked a hand through his hair and paced the small room like a caged animal. When he spotted Cole and Joey, he halted midstride.

Cole instantly squared his shoulders, ready to defend her if his half brother pounced.

"Let's all take a deep breath," Zane said as if he'd read the volatile situation and knew it needed to be diffused. He introduced Anna Wallace and Sheriff Carley Matheson to Cole, and Joey and the women spoke quietly, each reserved. From the reports, Cole knew that Joey had once shared a house for a short time with the Wallace sisters when they had all lived with Leland and Lou Anne. And she and Carley had grown up in the same town.

He was the biggest outsider of them all. Then again, Joey's father was in the hot seat now, placing her there along with him.

"Leland is holding Dad in a cabin here." Zane pointed to a map on the wall with a pushpin marking the location.

"What are his demands?" Zane asked.

"He's asked to speak to Joey. Says she's the only one he'll talk to."

"Absolutely not," Cole barked.

Joey cleared her throat. "He wants to speak to me. He gets me."

Cole brushed her arm with his hand. He'd almost lost her the day before. He wouldn't allow her to put herself in danger today. "Joey, please—"

"I know what I'm doing, Cole. Maybe I can talk some sense into him."

"We'll drive separate cars," Zane said. "Let's try to handle this without calling in a SWAT team."

Cole and Sloan agreed, and Sheriff Matheson checked her weapon as well. Two of the town's deputies were asked to follow but to wait for Zane's orders. Zane forced Anna to stay at the jail, and threatened to arrest Donna if she tried to interfere. They dispersed, taking different vehicles but agreeing to meet near the woods by the cabin and go in on foot. Fifteen minutes later they converged in a clearing with Zane taking the lead. Everyone was ordered to stay back until they learned Leland's demands.

Cole and his half brothers moved quietly with Joey beside him, the morning sun blistering hot as they hiked through the woods. When they reached a hill overlooking the small log cabin, Zane phoned inside.

"Mr. Hendricks. Lieutenant McKinney here." He gestured for Joey to make herself visible to the porch, and she stepped into the clearing.

"Joey is with us. Now tell us what you want."

He flipped the phone to speakerphone, and Leland's voice resonated over the line. "I'll release Jim McKinney in exchange for my freedom. I want you to drop all charges against me in the fake kidnapping/murder plan."

Cole exchanged furtive looks with Zane and Sloan.

"As Texas Rangers, we're required to enforce the law," Zane said. "We don't make deals with criminals, Mr. Hendricks."

The door creaked open and a crazed-looking Leland pushed Jim McKinney out onto the porch. He forced him to kneel and pressed a gun to the back of his head.

"Dad, let Mr. McKinney go," Joey shouted.

"He slept with Lou Anne. He started all of this years ago!"

Leland sounded distraught, as if he'd walked off a ledge. Joey started to go to him, but Cole held her back. "Wait. He's not rational, Joey."

Cole and Sloan followed Zane's cue and wove through the edges of the woods surrounding the house. Sloan to the right, Cole to the left.

"Convince them to drop the charges, Joey," Leland yelled. "You have power, Joey, you work for the governor."

"Why would Governor Grange agree to drop the charges?" Zane asked.

"Just get him here. He'll do it," Leland barked.

Cole had nearly reached the side of the house, and he hid in the bushes, waiting for Sloan to surface. Through the brush, he spotted his father on his knees. He thought

Jim would be scared, but he squared his shoulders, seemingly calm and resigned. Maybe he figured he deserved to die after the way he'd betrayed his wife and Cole's mother. And if he'd slept with Donna, if Justin was Jim's son, he had another son. Maybe he figured it was time he paid the price for that sin as well.

Cole's finger traced over the edge of his badge, then his hand moved to his pocket where he'd stored the one he'd found in the woods. The one he thought belonged to Jim.

Once upon a time his father had worn the badge proudly, too. Until he'd disgraced himself and his family. Still, he hadn't murdered the Wallace women.

Cole had thought he didn't care if the man lived or died. But faced with this dire situation, he realized he didn't want his father's punishment to be death.

He wanted to know the man who'd once worn that shield, to know if he still existed beneath the haggard surface. And although he'd been a poor excuse for a father, he deserved to have his professional name restored.

Sloan emerged from the brush across from him while Cole mentally formulated a diversion, but Joey suddenly shouted, then descended the hill, walking toward the house.

Leland yelled for her to stop, then stood and waved his gun in the air. Cole's blood ran cold. Dear God. Surely Leland wouldn't shoot his own daughter.

JOEY DARTED DOWN the hill, determined to stop Leland from hurting Jim McKinney.

"Let him go, Dad. Mr. McKinney had nothing to do with Lou Anne or Sarah's murder or the kidnapping."

"That may be true, but he humiliated me by having an affair with Lou Anne. He started the ruin of everything."

Joey was only inches from the porch now. She recognized the resignation in Jim's face. His wife was in a bad mental state, his sons' lives affected by his actions. And he had suffered for his wrongdoings. But he didn't deserve to die.

"I don't want to go to jail," Leland screeched. "Especially now I know your brother is alive. That Donna tricked me all these years."

"You never cared about Justin." Joey's voice caught. "I always wondered how you could plan to have him kidnapped. How you could use your own son to claim that insurance money."

"I was desperate then," Leland wailed. Sweat beaded and rolled down his face as he ranted and waved the gun in a wide arc.

"But you found out he wasn't your son," Joey said. "I understand now, Dad." She held up her hand, inching closer. From the corner of her eye, she saw Sloan on one side, Cole on the other.

Cole. Heavens, she loved him.

She pushed her own pain aside. Her family might never be whole again, but Cole deserved a chance to know the father he'd never had.

"Let Jim go," Joey said in a placating tone. "Please, Dad, it's time for the violence to end."

"I can't go to jail," Leland said in a panic. "I can't be shut away like some damn animal, Joey. You have to make the cops see that I didn't carry out that plan so they can't arrest me."

He hadn't carried it out because Rosa had beaten him to it. And now she'd suffer for her actions.

"You can arrange for me to be pardoned," Leland pleaded as he raised the gun toward her. "You work for Governor Grange. Arrange it for me, Joey."

Joey swallowed back her fear. "Let Jim go and I'll call him."

Leland aimed the gun at the back of Jim's head and shoved him down the steps. "Call him first."

Sloan inched from the bushes to reveal his location. "Leland, let my father go. Then we'll talk."

Leland's crazed look terrified Joey.

"You don't want to hurt Jim," Sloan said. "Not for an affair that happened sixteen years ago."

"Or does this have to do with Justin's father?" Cole asked.

Leland spun sideways. "You bastard. How can you protect this man here? He never cared about you."

"Just like you didn't care about Justin," Joey said sharply, dragging his gaze back to her.

He waved the gun back and forth between her and Cole, his hand shaking.

"But I'm your daughter, Dad. You won't shoot me, will you?" She took another step closer, and he jerked the gun toward Cole.

"I'll shoot him unless you call the governor right now! He'll give me a pardon."

"Why would he do that?" Cole asked.

"Because he's Justin's father," Leland yelled bitterly.

Shock registered on Cole's and Sloan's faces. Then Cole glanced at her with a question in his eyes, and she realized that he'd thought Jim might be Justin's father. Neither had trusted the other enough to tell the truth.

"But he's no better than Jim," Leland yelled. "He didn't want to break up his happy marriage or ruin his career. So he let Donna pawn the kid off as mine."

Joey's chest constricted as more emotions

pummeled her. How would Justin cope with this knowledge?

"Call him!" Leland bellowed.

Joey reached for her cell phone at the same moment Cole pounced toward Leland. Leland swung the gun sideways, and Joey lurched forward to stop Leland. She reached for the gun, but Jim McKinney slammed his hand into Leland's arm and sent the weapon flying into the dirt.

She hit the ground, while Cole grabbed Leland and hauled his arms behind him. Seconds later, he snapped handcuffs on her father, and Zane and Sloan rushed forward.

Tears rushed to her eyes at the sight of the Rangers arresting her father. Cole darted toward her, but she shook her head to warn him not to. She needed time to deal with the pain and shock. Time to regroup. Time to figure out how she'd break the news to her newfound brother.

And she still had to talk to the governor.

She glanced at Cole again. She loved him. But men couldn't be trusted. They cheated and lied and used you, then walked away.

So far, Cole hadn't cheated on her. And

she didn't know if he'd ever lied. But he would walk away. She knew that in her heart.

And she'd have to let him.

Chapter Sixteen

Cole drove Joey back to the courthouse in silence. Zane had taken custody of Leland and Jim rode with Sloan. The investigation was officially over.

And he was worried sick about Joey. She looked withdrawn, pale and obviously didn't want to talk. Having to snap those handcuffs on her father had been hell.

But at least he hadn't had to shoot Leland.

He'd been prepared to, though. If he'd harmed one hair on Joey's head…

His gut clenched as he parked, and he spotted the media circus on the lawn in front of the courthouse. Harold Dennison stood in front of the camera like a peacock strutting his feathers, and an official car that obviously belonged to the governor was parked in front. Oh, boy, the dog do was about to hit the fan.

"Joey, I'm sorry." He caught her hand as he parked.

"You did what you had to do, Cole." Her voice sounded flat, but Cole realized that she kept a tight rein on her emotions and didn't expect attention or sympathy.

All the more reason he wanted to hold her. She never asked for anything, but he instinctively sensed she needed comfort. Needed him.

Which made him feel even worse. He wished she'd yell at him. Hit him. Scream at him for hauling her father into jail. But this quiet acceptance was killing him.

The next few minutes chaos shadowed every moment. Zane and Sloan and the deputies arrived, along with Sheriff Matheson who helped to part the crowd of locals on the lawn and spirit the necessary parties inside.

Joey paused by the media cameras, and handled herself with a professional detachment as she briefly summarized the situation, answered and fended off questions. Of course, she carefully omitted any comment about Justin's paternity.

"What will happen to Rosa Ramirez and Leland Hendricks now?" Dennison asked.

Joey inhaled a deep breath. "Charges will be filed, court dates set. The town of Justice will finally have justice." She turned the mike back over to Dennison who began to comb the crowd for comments, and Cole whisked her inside.

Donna and Anna greeted them with exasperated but relieved looks.

Zane rushed in and Anna hugged him. "I'm glad your father is safe. And now maybe my mother and sister can rest in peace."

"And we can move on with our lives, finally," Zane said.

Governor Grange stood by the window looking out, seemingly lost in thought as he studied the curious mob outside.

Joey cleared her throat, and Cole touched her arm. "Would you like some privacy?"

She arched a brow toward the governor, but he shook his head. "It's going to be public record soon enough. Might as well get it over with."

"You're Justin's father?" Joey asked calmly.

He nodded and sank onto a bench. "How long have you known?"

"Not long." Joey glanced at Cole, then continued. "I saw your name in Lou Anne's date book, then when I met Justin, I suspected it was true."

"You had evidence you kept from us?" Zane asked.

"I just found it and didn't know if it was important," Joey argued.

Donna clasped her hands together, looking calmer than she had in ages, as if she was finally relieved to have everything in the open.

"You didn't want your family to know about your affair," Cole said, letting Joey off the hook. "You had to protect your political career."

He nodded in confirmation. "My wife knows everything now," he said. "I told her last night."

Joey folded her arms across her chest. "How is Martha taking the news that you lied to her for years and that you have a child?"

He shrugged. "Surprisingly well. She said she'd suspected something years ago. And she…thinks I should contact the boy." His gaze lifted to Joey's, and Cole saw a tired man. "What do you think, Joey?"

"I don't know. Maybe. Sometime. But Justin—Caleb—needs time. He's just learned that he's a part of our family." A mirthless laugh escaped her. "As twisted as it is. He has a lot to contemplate right now. I'm not even sure he wants to see me, and I didn't betray him."

Governor Grange nodded in acceptance and ran a hand through his thinning gray hair. "Of course I'll resign from office immediately."

"You don't have to do that, Clayton," Donna said. "You've done wonderful things for the state. People will understand."

He shifted and gave her an odd look. "You were always so rational under pressure, Donna. I admired that about you."

She patted his shoulder. "You were meant for office. If I hadn't known that was the best thing for you and the state, I wouldn't have kept your secret so long."

He flattened his hands on his knees. "Well, I suppose we'll see what the people think. How they feel. In the end, it'll be up to them."

"Is that why you sent me here?" Joey asked. "You wanted me to keep tabs on the investigation because of Justin?"

"That was partly it. I wanted answers about his death," the governor said. "But I also knew you'd do the right thing, Joey. You have integrity. I'm glad my son's alive and has you for a sister."

Zane appeared then with Jim in tow. The badge in Cole's pocket stabbed at his conscience. It was time to return it.

Zane waved them into a small office. Jim shoved a hand through his hair, looking harried, but his eyes brightened as he looked up at Sloan and Zane. Then he gave Cole a smile. "You boys are all good Rangers," he said. "I know I've let you down over the years, but I want you to know that I'm proud of all three of you. And I'm sorry I tore our family apart."

Cole shifted on the balls of his feet, feeling like an outsider again. He didn't belong here. Never would.

Still, he removed the badge from his pocket. "I found this in the woods that day I was searching for evidence."

Zane frowned. "You withheld evidence."

Sloan made a sound of surprise. "You knew it belonged to our father."

Cole nodded. "I wanted to check it out first."

"You mean you wanted to investigate me?" Jim said with quiet acceptance.

Cole met the man's gaze head-on. "I didn't know if you were innocent or guilty."

"I told the truth," Jim said. "I didn't remember what happened that night. But I must have lost my badge when I was drunk, after I left Lou Anne."

"We know you didn't kill her," Sloan said. "That's what matters, Dad."

"No." Jim threw up a hand. "I made a mess of things years ago. I cheated on your mother and disgraced myself with the Rangers." His expression turned grave as he slanted his gaze toward Cole. "But most of all, I let your brother down."

A knot gathered in Cole's throat.

"I kept up with you, though, Cole," he said in a gruff tone. "All these years, I knew what you were doing. Where you were. And before your mother died—"

"She died still loving you," Cole said bitterly. "I never understood that. Not when you didn't return her love. Not when you didn't even bother to attend her funeral or acknowledge that you had a third son."

"You're wrong about my feelings," Jim said with more force. "I did love your mother, Cole. I…considered leaving Stella for her more than once. But I had my other two sons to think of." He gestured toward Sloan and Zane. "I'm sorry, boys. Sorry for loving another woman. But Stella …she was weak. The love just dwindled after a while."

"But you stayed with her," Zane said.

"She needed me." Jim faced Cole. "Your mother, Barb, was strong. I knew she'd be all right. Stella wouldn't have survived. Besides…" He rubbed a hand down his leg. "I'd already screwed up by cheating, and losing my badge. If I could do one honorable thing, it would be to honor my wedding vows to my legal wife. And I was afraid if I divorced her, she might commit suicide."

Cole had hated Jim McKinney for so long, that it was hard to let go of the bitterness. But he was a man now, not a boy, and he recognized the truth in his father's words. Some semblance of admiration stirred that even though his father had strayed, he had stuck to his marriage commitment.

He handed the badge to his father and then shook his hand. It wasn't a perfect start, wouldn't compensate for the isolation and lost years, but it was a beginning.

At least they finally had justice.

Zane, then Sloan, shook Cole's hand as well. "Thanks for holding onto Dad's badge," Zane said.

"And for returning it," Sloan said.

Cole nodded, feeling a bond being forged, as if they were finally welcoming him into their brotherhood.

But what about Joey—could she forgive him for his part in arresting her father?

And was there a possibility that she hadn't just muttered that she loved him in the heat of their passion-frenzied lovemaking, but that she'd meant the sentiment? That they might really have something together?

JOEY EXITED the courthouse, her heart in her throat. Cole and his father and brothers were finally reconciling. Cole would have the family he deserved.

While her family still remained in shreds, totally dysfunctional. Maybe someday Justin would come around, and at least she and he could have a relationship.

Weary and still reeling from the fact that Governor Grange had fathered her brother, she walked toward the bar. A drink would help wash away the pain. Help her get her act together. Force her to prepare for saying goodbye to Cole.

The lunch crowd had filled the parking lot, and Joey was just about to go inside when the sound of a Harley ripping toward her jerked her attention away from the door. Her pulse clamored as Cole skidded toward her. His blue eyes skated over her from head to toe, then his gaze settled on her face.

Her heart capitulated as disappointment

ballooned inside her chest. He was leaving town already. Going to ride away and she'd never see him again. Never have his lips on her. Feel his touch. Have him inside her.

Hell, it was better. Men were cheaters, liars and then they walked away.

Or in this case, sped away on a Hog.

"Hey, legs. Thought you might like a ride?"

Temptation thrummed through her. But why stall the inevitable? Better to make a clean break than draw out the pain. "Thanks, but I don't want to hold you up."

His brows shot up. "Hold me up?"

"You're leaving town, aren't you?"

He shrugged, and she remembered how it felt to rest her head on those broad shoulders. "Eventually."

Unwanted tears collected in her suddenly dry throat. "I need a drink."

He patted the bag slung over the back of the bike. "We can take Jose with us. Have a threesome."

"Sounds kinky."

He wiggled his brows. "Might be. I have

salt and lime, and know some inventive ways to use them."

A small smile tugged at her mouth as titillating sensations splintered through her. Memories of their first meeting crashed back, then their lovemaking. His teasing comment about watching her suck the lime and wanting her mouth on him.

But one ride with him would only make her crave another. And then she might break down and make a fool out of herself by begging him not to leave.

"Cole…"

His expression grew serious, and he reached for her hand and tugged her close, so that she rested against him. "I know you think that all men are liars and cheaters…"

"They are."

He traced a path along her cheek with his thumb. "And that they use you and then walk away—"

"They do." Although she ached for things to be different.

He pulled her hand to his mouth and pressed a kiss to each finger. "I promise not to cheat or lie to you, Joey."

She pushed at his shoulders, needing distance before she broke down and cried and begged him to love her. "Maybe not, but—"

"No buts." A smoldering intensity underscored his words, and he tightened his grip, refusing to let her run. "And I'm not walking away, sugar."

A tear trickled down her cheek. She desperately wanted to believe him. "Our families, Cole…our history. Look at them."

"We're not *them*," he said thickly. "Give us a chance, Joey. We can make our own family the way we want it."

Hope slivered through her. What was he saying?

"Family?"

He threaded his fingers through her hair and yanked her down across his lap. "I love you, sugar."

"Cole—"

He pressed a finger over her lips to shush her. "I love you, and I want to marry you."

Joey stared into his eyes, his words echoing in her head. Sincerity mingled with heat and passion in his eyes. A passion that she had known with only one man. A love she'd felt when she'd been in his arms and no one else's.

He had whispered the words in return. And he'd sounded as if he meant them.

"Now, don't make me beg." Emotions thickened his voice. "I almost lost you before, Joey. I don't want to lose you again. Not ever."

"I don't want to lose you, either," she whispered.

"Then climb on, sugar," he said with a sexy smile twisting his lips, "and let's go for that ride."

"Where are we going?" she asked breathlessly.

He grinned and swung her around until she climbed on behind him. "Someplace where we can be alone, and I can feel those mile-long legs wrapped around me."

She nuzzled his neck with her tongue. "Someplace where I can sprinkle that salt and lime juice on your body and lick it off?"

"Oh, yeah, sugar. Someplace where we can make all those fantasies I've been having about you come true."

She clasped her hands around his waist

and leaned into him. He had already made all her dreams come true just by loving her. But a shot of tequila off his washboard belly and his length inside her was definitely another fantasy to look forward to.

And she was certain that they could think of others…

* * * * *

Turn the page for a sneak preview of
IF I'D NEVER KNOWN YOUR LOVE
by
Georgia Bockoven

From the brand-new series
Harlequin Everlasting Love
Every great love has a story to tell.™

One year, five months and four days missing

There's no way for you to know this, Evan, but I haven't written to you for a few months. Actually, it's been almost a year. I had a hard time picking up a pen once more after we paid the second ransom and then received a letter saying it wasn't enough. I was so sure you were coming home that I took the kids along to Bogotá so they could fly home with you and me, something I swore I'd never do. I've fallen in love with Colombia and the people who've opened their hearts to me. But fear is a constant companion when I'm there. I won't ever expose our children to that kind of danger again.

I'm at a loss over what to do anymore, Evan. I've begged and pleaded and thrown temper tantrums with every official I can corner both here and at home. They've been incredibly tolerant and understanding, but in the end as ineffectual as the rest of us.

I try to imagine what your life is like now, what you do every day, what you're wearing, what you eat. I want to believe that the people who have you are misguided yet kind, that they treat you well. It's how I survive day to day. To think of you being mistreated hurts too much. If I picture you locked away somewhere and suffering, a weight descends on me that makes it almost impossible to get out of bed in the morning.

Your captors surely know you by now. They have to recognize what a good man you are. I imagine you working with their children, telling them that you have children, too, showing them the pictures you carry in your wallet. Can't the men who have you understand how much your children miss you? How can it not matter to them?

How can they keep you away from us all this time? Over and over, we've done what they asked. Are they oblivious to the depth of their cruelty? What kind of people are they that they don't care?

I used to keep a calendar beside our bed next to the peach rose you picked for me before you left. Every night I marked another day, counting how many you'd been gone. I don't do that any longer. I don't want to be reminded of all the days we'll never get back.

When I can't sleep at night, I tell you about my day. I imagine you hearing me and smiling over the details that make up my life now. I never tell you how defeated I feel at moments or how hard I work to hide it from everyone for fear they will see it as a reason to stop believing you are coming home to us.

And I couldn't tell you about the lump I found in my breast and how difficult it was going through all the tests without you here to lean on. The lump was benign—the process reaching that diagnosis utterly terrifying. I couldn't stop thinking about what would happen to Shelly and Jason if something happened to me.

We need you to come home.

I'm worn down with missing you.

I'm going to read this tomorrow and will probably tear it up or burn it in the fireplace. I don't want you to get the idea I ever doubted what I was doing to free you or thought the work a burden. I would gladly spend the rest of my life at it, even if, in the end, we only had one day together.

You are my life, Evan.

I will love you forever.

* * * * *

Don't miss this deeply moving
Harlequin Everlasting Love story
about a woman's struggle to bring back her
kidnapped husband from Colombia and
her turmoil over whether to let go, finally,
and welcome another man into her life.
IF I'D NEVER KNOWN YOUR LOVE
by Georgia Bockoven
is available March 27, 2007.

And also look for
THE NIGHT WE MET
by Tara Taylor Quinn,
a story about finding love
when you least expect it.

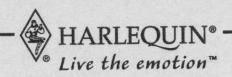
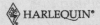

HARLEQUIN®
INTRIGUE®

BREATHTAKING ROMANTIC SUSPENSE

Shared dangers and passions lead to electrifying
romance and heart-stopping suspense!

Every month, you'll meet six new heroes
who are guaranteed to make your spine tingle
and your pulse pound. With them you'll enter
into the exciting world of Harlequin Intrigue—
where your life is on the line
and so is your heart!

THAT'S INTRIGUE—
ROMANTIC SUSPENSE
AT ITS BEST!

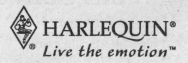

HARLEQUIN®
Live the emotion™

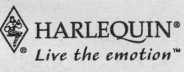

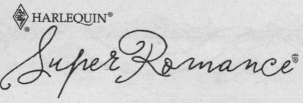

HARLEQUIN®

Super Romance®

...there's more to the story!

Superromance.
A *big* satisfying read about unforgettable
characters. Each month we offer *six* very different
stories that range from family drama to adventure
and mystery, from highly emotional stories to
romantic comedies—and much more! Stories
about people you'll believe in and care about.
Stories too compelling to put down....

Our authors are among today's *best* romance
writers. You'll find familiar names and talented
newcomers. Many of them are award winners—
and you'll see why!

If you want the biggest and best
in romance fiction, you'll get it
from Superromance!

Exciting, Emotional, Unexpected...

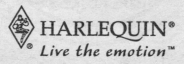

HARLEQUIN®
Live the emotion™

Harlequin® Historical
Historical Romantic Adventure!

Imagine a time of chivalrous knights and unconventional ladies, roguish rakes and impetuous heiresses, rugged cowboys and spirited frontierswomen— these rich and vivid tales will capture your imagination!

Harlequin Historical... they're too good to miss!